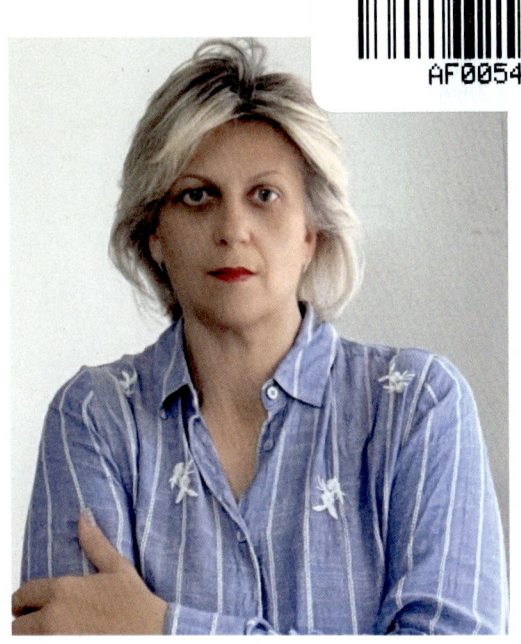

My real name is Maryann Zahra, but I also go by the pen name Maryann Ring Spencer. I was born in Malta and currently reside not far from Villa Sans Souci. I was inspired to create this book by this villa, its history, and the history of our islands. In this book, I've highlighted Florence Nightingale's thoughts on feminism and the visits Florence Nightingale made to our islands. The idea that the word 'equality' should never have been, is one in which I firmly believe!

Villa Sans Souci

Maryann Ring Spencer

Villa Sans Souci

Vanguard Press

VANGUARD PAPERBACK

© Copyright 2024
Maryann Ring Spencer

The right of Maryann Ring Spencer to be identified as
author of this work has been asserted by her in accordance
with the
Copyright, Designs and Patents Act 1988.

All Rights Reserved

No reproduction, copy or transmission of this publication
may be made without written permission.
No paragraph of this publication may be reproduced,
copied or transmitted save with the written permission of
the publisher, or in accordance with the provisions of the
Copyright Act 1956 (as amended).

Any person who commits any unauthorised act in
relation to this publication may be liable to criminal
prosecution and civil claims for damages.

A CIP catalogue record for this title is available from the British Library.

ISBN 978 1 83794 105 6

This is a work of fiction. Names, characters, businesses, places, events, and
incidents are either the product of the author's imagination or used in a fictitious
manner. Any resemblance to actual persons, living or dead, or actual events is
purely coincidental

Vanguard Press is an imprint of
Pegasus Elliot Mackenzie Publishers Ltd.
www.pegasuspublishers.com

First Published in 2024
Vanguard Press
Sheraton House Castle Park
Cambridge England

Printed & Bound in Great Britain

For the late Her Majesty Queen Elizabeth II,
who loved our Maltese Islands

I owe my profoundest thanks to Christopher Zahra, my husband, who always encourages me and supports me in all my dreams. I also thank the production team at Pegasus, who have been of great assistance in publishing this book.

Scene on back cover depicts the fishing village of Marsaxlokk (Marsascirocco)

Artist: Anthony Patrick Vella

PROLOGUE

Villa Sans Souci

1891, Marsascirocco, Malta

A doleful, uneasy sequence of *ding-dongs* cut through the silence of the waning crescent moon night and reached the ears of the smartly dressed sergeant-in-charge. He jumped to his feet, calling two other police officers with just a glance of his eyes, and commanding them to hastily move on to their usual duties.

The sound of the bell was coming from the mansion of Doctor Salvatore Luigi Pisani, Villa Sans Souci, situated between Casal Zejtun and Marsascirocco, its name reflecting the courage of character he managed to build up in his profession, that of a 'carefree' attitude, which he maintained even in the worst situations he confronted during the war.

The mansion, bristling with fine architectural features on the outside and overlooking the fields and vineyards, had more luxury to offer on the inside. The interior was focused on a large central hallway serving as the hub leading to the adjacent rooms. Rooms with sixteen-foot ceilings were decorated with frescoes depicting the romantic Victorian era.

The predominant colours were dark with tan and gold highlights in one room, creating an interesting contrast to the other rooms' frescoes of pinks, pale blues, tans, and black detailing; a combination of colours repeated throughout the floors of the house. The fireplace of one room stood on the west wall and that of the other room on the east wall. Both were constructed with Maltese limestone, one decorated with beautifully sculpted sea waves and dolphins and the other with branches and lion heads. One could almost hear the roar from their delicately sculpted details.

The tall windows, Queen Anne and Victorian style, were banded at the top by a panel of coloured lights. These were blue, amber, purple, and red, and gave enough light to illuminate all four corners during daylight, whereas in the evening, both rooms sparkled under the chic crystal candle chandeliers, multiplying their brilliant glittering coloured rainbow candle-light over the decorative tiled floors, the old aristocratic furniture, and all the accoutrements of the home owner's wealth and social standing, his intelligence, his devotion to family and religion, and his acceptance of new and modern ideas—all demonstrated without a single word being spoken. The dark oak polished doors with decorative accents on the frames and heavy polished brass hinges and knobs added that extra elegance to the rooms.

Continuing down the hallway, on the right side was the formal dining room, with a huge chevalier oak table in the centre, ready to host thirty guests or more. Sideboards were decorated with silver candelabra, crystal glasses, and blue Wedgewood dinnerware. The dining room had panel doorways on the west wall, one of which opened to the pantry and continued to the kitchen, and the other door opened to a small storage area and a spiral staircase to the wine cellar.

In addition to serving as the entranceway for the main rooms of entertainment, the hallway also served as a grand entrance to the rooms above. The walls of the staircase were adorned with frescoes of vibrant blue to denote the importance of the blue sea that surrounds the Maltese islands and the picturesque fishing village of Marsascirocco.

The main stairways' elaborateness was evident. Attached to the sides of the risers were the balustrades connected by a sculpted banister. The staircase was open to the first-floor level, with a landing in between that featured large arched windows overlooking the mansion's garden. Upon reaching the first-floor landing, the balustrade formed a balcony overlooking the hallway, forming two arches. Each arch had a forged iron gate to separate this part of the house from the rest in case unwanted visitors eventually made it inside.

The first floor had bedrooms, one of which had access through an ancillary hallway to another room always under lock, visited only by Dr Pisani himself, as it held his treasure of collectible medals and other riches. The bedrooms' furniture was practically alike: dark oak style with marble tops and a standing mirror framed in a sculpted ornamental border. The balcony door of each bedroom led to a common terrace structured with engraved Roman pillars. An exception was one of the bedrooms on the west side of the hallway, as it was decorated and had more elaborate furniture, with a four-poster bed facing the main balcony and heavy damask curtains. It was used for important guests or family members wishing to spend a night at this mansion. A door leading into a viaduct that connects to a portion of the house that seems to be a separate house all on its own was located next to the west side wall of the hallway. It led onto two sizable rooms that were primarily used as workshops or storage spaces. Huge hooks were hung on the rooms' four walls, and a hefty wooden barn door opened into a narrow spiral staircase that descended into a vast, empty chamber for animals. It has symmetrically placed doors and windows, as well as a hayloft. Drainage channels were located along the sides of the brick floors. These were the stables. An archway opened to reveal a vast, lush garden full of peach and citrus trees, flowers, and other plants. The garden was peaceful and serene, especially at the limestone gazebo that was its focal point and provided a view of Marsascirocco.

Returning to the main stairs on the first floor level, it continued to the second floor level, where on the west side was a large room with a library, a writing desk, and a stunning floral carpeting. A restroom and a laundry room with metal, huge washtubs and possers were located on the east side of this floor.

A narrower and simpler stairway ascended to the roof from the second floor. Up there, there was ample space, with views of Marsascirocco stretching from one side of the coastline to the other. It was a stunning panoramic vista that included the shore of this fishing village as well as the green meadows. This view was only obstructed on the villa's front side by a niche. This was built so that a large bell could be hung and used as the sole means of contact with the neighbourhood's residents and law enforcement.

The sergeant and his assistants pulled the reins of their galloping horses as soon as they got close to the professor's mansion. With the help of his strong physique, the sergeant was able to leap off the beast before coming to a complete halt. Holding on to the horse, he avoided falling to the ground and managed to stay standing. He hurried to knock on the front door, which he discovered to be ajar, leaving the horse in the care of the other police officers.

'Dr Pisani, Dr Pisani!' The sergeant called out as he snuck into the hallway.

The doctor retorted, 'I'm up here, behind the gates. Someone broke inside; I heard a windowpane crash, so someone might be wandering down there.'

The sergeant opened the drawing room door while holding a truncheon in his right hand, and one of the police officers followed him while holding a five-candle silver candelabrum that he picked from a shelf next to the door.

'We will have a thorough look around; you just stay safe up there,' suggested the sergeant.

They searched inside the house, the stables, and the garden, but to no avail. The third police officer, who stayed outside, had a quick look around the house. It was pitch black, but with just the help of a dim street oil lamp and a match that he lit up, looking for either a poor, ragged boy or a skilled thief, he didn't see any suspicious movements. They found the broken glass pieces scattered on the floor of the drawing room and half a muddy footprint on the path outside the entrance door, but there was no sign of anyone.

'There's no one inside; it seems that the thief ran away,' affirmed the sergeant, 'but I will leave one of my police officers here in the hallway for the night.'

'I'm very grateful for your assistance,' replied Dr Pisani.

'However, leave the forged iron gate closed for double security,' suggested the sergeant to the professor.

'And you,' continued the sergeant, tapping his truncheon on his white-gloved palm, 'heap the broken scattered glass in that corner for now and lock up the wooden shutters that were left open.'

'Yes, sir,' replied the police officer. After following the sergeant's orders, he positioned himself behind the main door, guarding the front entrance of the mansion until the break of dawn.

CHAPTER ONE

The Merry Life

1838, Paris

Along the streets of Paris, the luxurious landaus and the horses' hooves trampled the grungy roads and stopped in front of rich mansions. The women's heels echoed in the silence of the night as they made their way towards these carriages, wearing resplendent, fashionable gowns and accompanied by their husbands, other family members, or friends.

'*Bonsoir*,' said the footmen while helping the ladies climb into the carriage. After making sure everyone was sitting comfortably, he signalled to the coachman to drive off.

'You are going to a debutante ball tonight, my dears,' Fanny conveyed to both her daughters whilst arranging her dress on the seat of the carriage. 'You need to 'come out' and be presented to society.'

Florence and Parthe gave a glance to each other and stretched their lips in a sort of smile while hiding behind their mother-of-pearl-decorated fans, which they had been fanning in front of their faces to cool themselves.

Florence Nightingale and her sister, Parthe, were both charming young ladies. This was not their first ball; on the contrary, they had attended so many that they were among the best dancers. Gentlemen went crazy for them, and once they received so many invitations to dance at a ball that they were too exhausted to make it to the horse-drawn carriage to go home. They knew the fanology by heart, and the most used by Florence and Parthe was putting the fan half open on their faces, meaning that they were being watched, and it was true, as their mother always kept her eyes on them, knowing that she possessed two beautiful daughters.

Operas, gatherings, balls, and concerts made up the Nightingales' daily schedule. A gay and attractive life, with a consistent pattern both here in Paris and elsewhere. Fanny, their energetic mother, always aspired to be in the limelight wherever they went. She detested just hanging out in the background without any chance to shine.

In the Place Vendôme, in the centre of Paris, the Nightingales stayed in a richly decorated apartment.

'We're lucky to be living this luxurious life, aren't we?' Parthe inquired as she cast a sidelong glance at her sister, who was peering out of the carriage window.

Florence responded, 'My eyes are always wide open to what is going on around us, not like your selfish attitude. If I were to turn the clock back and be born again, I would prefer to have been in a family where I used less of my time in this extravagant life.'

'Ah! See, mum, she's referring to me as selfish once more.'

Their mother continued to gaze out of the carriage window while maintaining a straight back, focusing more on the infinitely dark sky and having thoughts of the glitzy evening ahead of her.

'Can't you see what I'm seeing? There are filthy, hungry people asking for food or trying to sleep on both sides of the street. Who can tell if they are ill or how much agony they are experiencing?'

'Who cares? So, why should I care?' Parthe responded.

'And look, drunken men relieving themselves wherever they are; this is insane, this is poor hygiene, this will mean diseases.'

'But we are wealthy, we are clean, and we are scented,' concluded Parthe.

In front of the enormous private estate, Château du Rousseau, the carriage came to a stop. This imposing Renaissance-style château, which dominated the Gironde Estuary and reigned over vineyards producing delicate grand vin for the guests, had broken its silence and welcomed dancing, laughter, and amusing anecdotes inside its splendour.

'Who invited us here?' Florence questioned her mother.

'Miss Mary Clarke,' Fanny said, smiling at the footman who reached out to help her get out of the coach.

The young ladies were light in their steps and didn't need the footman's help. Quickening her step, Florence's voice reached her mother's ears from behind.

'And who is this, Miss Mary Clarke?'

'Don't you remember? We met her already at the celebrities' fête last week, and I told you that she is a major figure in politics,' answered her mother.

'Ah, that woman, she really liked us; is she a woman in parliament?'

'Don't make me laugh, Flo; have you ever heard of a woman sitting in parliament?'

'So why did you say a major figure in politics?'

'She founded and runs an intellectual salon, where she meets significant individuals and maintains significant contacts. Don't ask me any more questions, Flo; we're meeting the other guests right now.'

Florence's parents, William and Fanny, were the first to enter the hallway, followed by their daughters. They were welcomed by Miss Mary Clarke.

The ballroom was lavishly furnished with enormous chandeliers, thick gold-framed wall mirrors, and ceiling paintings of dancing couples and contented lovers in private, peaceful gardens. A quartet played waltzes and polkas on one side of the ballroom. All the invitees' extravagant attire, particularly those worn by the women, revealed their high social position.

It didn't take long for Florence and Parthe's beauty to draw the attention of two gentlemen who invited them to dance. The daughters nodded their heads in agreement right away and accepted after giving their mother a quick glance.

After the dance, Florence grinned at her partner and left. She slipped outside via an open side door that led to a garden terrace decked with roses in a variety of hues, for she needed some fresh air, peace, and quiet. She was soothed by the aroma of the roses and took deep breaths till she heard someone calling her name, 'Florence, my dear.'

Florence was startled as she heard that voice and turned to say, 'Hello, Miss Clarke.'

Florence's appearance contrasted with Miss Clarke's. Clarkey, as she was often known by the Nightingales, was very scruffy; her hair was curly and ruffled, and she preferred to flaunt her amazing charm rather than dress decently.

'Are you tired?'

'No, not at all,' Florence said as she turned her head to look at the blooms.

'I chose to come out here and talk to someone with knowledge and common sense,' Mary Clarke remarked.

Mary Clarke's eyes met Florence's as she turned her head to look at her. The ballroom was crowded to the gills as Mary Clarke peered inside to see if someone might be keeping an eye on them.

'It's a special evening for me to see you again,' Mary Clarke murmured, gazing Florence in the eyes.

'I feel the same,' Florence replied.

'Shall we sit on the bench? My feet are killing me,' complained Miss Clarke, and before Florence could respond positively, she felt Miss Clarke's arm encircle her right arm as they paced towards a bench in a corner and sat down.

'You are aware of your remarkable qualities,' Miss

Clarke added.

Florence looked at Miss Clarke, who took Florence's hand in hers and caressed her palm.

'Flo, I normally don't like English women or women in general because of their foolish, closed-minded reasoning and speech. Men who are more educated and converse practically about everything are people I prefer to be with. But last Friday, when I first met you, you stunned me with your knowledge, the topics you discussed, and your overwhelmingly kind nature. I was impressed with your intelligence; your family gave you a good education in a variety of disciplines that are typically taught solely to men and not to women.'

'I'm delighted you like all of my family,' Florence responded, 'and I'm glad I met you since I'm sure I'll learn a lot from you in the short time we'll be here. I'm determined to meet influential people and soak up all the knowledge I can.'

'I will be happy to open doors for you, dear Flo. I will show you around Paris while you are here and introduce you to everyone who is significant.'

Such remarks made Florence's eyes gleam. She was aware that Mary Clarke truly meant everything she said.

CHAPTER TWO

Return to London

1839, Paris and Hampshire

On a wintry, chilly evening, the Nightingales gathered as a family in the warmth of the old, lavishly decorated fireplace, crackling with its cherry wood logs and creating dancing tongues of flame while leaving a relaxing aroma in the air. The silence in the room was broken by the voice of William, a loving family father with a keen interest in politics, a lover of books, and an aesthete of art.

'We're returning to Hampshire, but since the house renovations haven't been finished yet, we'll stay in London first. I need to check on how the work at Embley is going, though, to determine if any adjustments need to be made.'

'Sure, I look forward to returning to my Embley house, but before I go, I need to make sure that all of the interior décor and furniture have been installed as we had hoped, particularly the tapestries and rugs that I had ordered to be woven especially for us,' remarked Fanny.

'When are we leaving?' asked Florence.

William responded, 'We will arrive in London sometime in April. Next week, we embark on the voyage.' 'I will miss Paris,' added Parthe.

'We will miss the people, and we will cry again,' prompted Florence.

William retorted, 'But we need to move on, ladies. We cannot remain travelling, and we cannot remain here.'

'We need to finally settle down at our house,' said their mother, while stretching her arm for a cup of tea that one of the servants had just served.

Florence was sure to miss Paris, especially given her 'passion' for Mary Clarke. She had made many friends and learned a great deal about political issues and global concerns through her, but she also yearned to return home soon. She was conscious of what she later referred to as 'the call,' which she was considering to be the purpose of her life. It was clear that she was anxious about whether she would hear God speak to her again. Florence was troubled by the frivolous lifestyle she was leading. She had always thought that she needed to avoid social events like balls, theatre, and parties since she wouldn't hear from God during those times.

The journey from Paris to London began in April. Long rides in horse-drawn carriages on rough, jarring roads were uncomfortable. Anxiety was felt during deep, narrow passageways where all that could be heard were the hooves and rumbling wheels thundering on the rocky, potholed, and uneven surfaces, along with the creaking and squealing of tree branches and the rustling of leaves. The melody was made by the breezing winds, which occasionally blew hard and created clouds of dust that made it difficult to see what was outside the carriage windows.

Life for the Nightingales in London was much the same as it was in Paris. After attending the Queen's birthday party, they began a life of pleasure that included socialising with friends, chit-chatting, laughing, dancing, and banquets. Since their house in Hampshire still needed renovations, they temporarily relocated to central London, where their jovial lifestyle continued. This time, Florence completely forgot about her call and became 'passionate' about Marianne Nicholson, her cousin.

Every evening, music filled the air in the Nicholsons' luxuriously furnished corridor. Marianne had a beautiful carol-singing voice and a stunningly glamorous appearance. Marianne and Florence got along great together. They cherished one another. They were aware of their beauty as ladies. In Marianne's room, they used to spend a lot of time together talking about life and one another.

'No one will beat our beauty,' Marianne chuckled to Florence after sipping some thick brandy that late afternoon.

'Put that *eau de vie* away; it's not good for your angel voice,' Florence said, trying to grab the glass from Marianne's grip as she swayed from left to right.

Marianne grabbed Florence's wrist firmly as her hand was about to reach the glass, drank the last little from it, and then flung the empty glass to the ground. Her inebriated behaviour was jocular and overly cheerful. She fixed her gaze on Florence's eyes and drew her closer, gave her a hard hug, and kissed her on the cheek while saying in Florence's ears, 'We're too beautiful, too much.'

'I know,' Florence replied. 'Our extreme beauty is too superb to be wasted on men,' she said, looking into Marianne's eyes.

Before tears began to fall down their flawless faces, they embraced one another firmly in silence, the most loved moment of all. They gave each other a tender lip kiss after regaining their own presence in each other's gaze. Marianne let go of Florence's waist and wiped her tears with her thumb as she looked out the open window at the outside landscape.

'You have no idea what I see with my own eyes when I am in the theatre performing, and you have no idea what I see when I am backstage,' she sobbed. 'It's unfair how we're treated, unfair that all we're expected to do is look like prostitutes—is that the only occupation we can get outside of marriage? Is that our only right?'

Florence made an effort to calm her down. She understood what Marianne was alluding to. Women were treated extremely unfairly in a society that was created by men for men, with women only being valued as prostitutes or as subservient spouses and mothers.

'Poor ballerinas,' Marianne continued, 'every time the curtain closes after their performance, wealthy men, most of them elderly, come backstage among the ballerinas, to observe closely, stare closely at their bare arms and shoulders, touch their legs, and engage in sensual touches. Most of the men then choose a ballerina and take her away with them, and...'

'Don't go on,' Florence growled angrily as she punched a silk cushion. 'All these things make me angry, very angry.'

At this point, Florence heard God's call again. She needed to do something about all this: all this prostitution, misery, sickness, poverty, lack of sanitation and education, and so on. An endless list, a huge wave of social anxieties, diseases, and poverty–but when to start and from where? How can she, a beautiful, charming lady, start addressing all these issues?

'I'm hating myself for being female!' shouted Marianne, kicking the glass she had fallen earlier on the floor.

'No, don't say that; we need to start a revolution; we need to start somewhere; the world is waiting for us to start this change; the world is suffocating by men's primitive, egoistic, and unloving outrage towards women who are aware of sexual sufferings leading to sicknesses, mental disorders, and lack of sanitation, and you know it's endless, and more and more of us are receiving no assistance when we're sick,' said Florence, trying to calm Marianne by grasping Marianne's shoulder from behind.

'You're a dreamer, Flo; you don't know what you're saying.'

'I know this is like fighting an evil beast, but I'm not going to allow males to ruin our lives any longer. They think they are above everything, but I see that not all men are to blame for what's happening in our world,' said Florence while heading towards the door.

'Most of them?' prompted Marianne.

Florence put her hand on the doorknob and said, 'Thanks to Mary Clarke, I found some good gentlemen that I can work shoulder to shoulder with.'

'You're leaving me?' Marianne asked. 'I don't feel well.'

'If I were you, I would take a nap; all you need is a good rest after all that drinking. I'll be in the front row in the theatre tomorrow, watching you and admiring you. I swear.'

After leaving Marianne's suite, Florence went directly to her room, shut the door behind her, and sat down at her desk with her face buried in her hands.

'Oh God, help! Am I in love? I don't know.' She took the diary out of the desk drawer. Writing down her experiences before going to bed was a daily practice for her.

'Oh, God, am I in love with my cousin?'

She grabbed her pen, dipped it in ink, and wrote, 'I never loved but one person with passion in my life, and that is her, Marianne.'

CHAPTER THREE

The Call to Service

1839–1842, Hampshire

The Nightingales moved into their renovated Hampshire home in the autumn of 1839. The interior of the home was filled with elegant furniture, silk, damask, tapestries, and expensive woven rugs. Fanny was quite pleased. The following phase involved hiring the household, ladies' maids, a footman, two waiters, two housemaids, three laundry maids, and a cook.

Florence was desperate. There was emptiness in her life without Marianne. She also felt unwell since she had put no effort into answering her 'call,' which was upsetting.

She was locking herself in her room and spending a lot of time writing in her diary and taking notes. When she wrote, she was attempting to relieve her stress, but it was insufficient. She needed assistance, which she was able to get from her Aunt Mai, a sensible and logical woman who had arrived at Embley for the Christmas celebrations. Since Florence trusted her aunt, she immediately confided in her.

'I told Mary Clarke in a letter that I wanted to study advanced mathematics rather than just the basics that my father had taught me, and she agreed that I should continue my education. However, I'm not sure how I'm going to tell my mother about it.'

Instead of performing routine tasks for women and putting any effort into learning music, which she disliked, Florence wanted her mind to operate in cognitive methods, logical concepts, mathematics, and statistics.

'I will speak to your mother, my dear,' Aunt Mai assured her.

However, all hell broke loose when Aunt Mai commanded Fanny to locate a mathematician.

'What does she need mathematics for? She should be thinking about marriage, not mathematics, and what about the regular housework?' countered Florence's mother.

Aunt Mai retorted, 'Listen, your reasoning shows that you have no idea what there is in your daughter at all.'

After a few weeks, Aunt Mai's persistence paid off, and Fanny's brother was appointed Florence's mathematics professor.

Meanwhile, Fanny carried on with her merry life of gatherings, banquets, plays, and social celebrity interactions. She brought Parthe and Florence along so that they could socialise with people of prominent standing. Florence was highly regarded everywhere she went for her remarkable intelligence. She was able to talk and start a discussion with anyone, including a chevalier, duke, ambassador, or other powerful political figures.

Florence and Richard Monckton Milnes met for the first time during a dinner Florence's father held in Embley's formal dining room in celebration of the poet John Keats. Richard had achieved enormous success in London society, was trusted with the first collection and publication of the well-known poet Keats and was also expected to have a big political career. He discovered from Florence that they had a lot in common when it came to their love of humanitarian work, especially with children.

'So, in addition to writing your own poems, you have been trusted with the works of the famous John Keats; isn't that an honour?' inquired Florence.

'Oh, a true honour; he was the best romantic poet, a genius in his writings, and working on some of his greatest works of literature has elevated me in the literary world.'

'Doing what you enjoy doing is not work; it is merely pleasure.'

'As my friend John Keats so eloquently put it, it's a real pleasure. When I consider how great poetry is, how much may be acquired from it, and what a thing it is to be in the mouth of fame, I often wonder why I should be a poet more than other men.'

'If fame makes you happy, what about politics?'

Every new person Florence Nightingale met was the subject of extensive questions. She was always thinking about what help that individual could give her in the future.

'The Young England Party is asking for my support, but my views are very different from theirs.'

'So, only poems?'

'No, I'm worried about the situation in Ireland. As you may know, famine is at its worst.'

'Not only in Ireland, but also in our community and beyond.'

'I feel bad that we're rich, and then I go outside and see poverty. I regret the young souls whom I assist or try to assist; at the very least, I do something, but I feel as if I am doing nothing.'

'We must start somewhere, right? Every little bit of assistance matters.'

Richard made regular visits to Embley during that summer. He frequently discussed his charitable undertakings with Florence, and he started to feel attracted to her—or at least he thought so—as though she were a member of the family. Richard's emotions, though, were hazy. One afternoon, while they wandered around the estate, enjoying the sun on their faces, Richard asked Florence, 'Do you love me?'

'I have too much on my mind,' Florence said, looking bewildered and experiencing a rush of blood to her face.

'Will you marry me?'

'No, no, hold on. I'm not sure. I'm not sowing a marriage relationship here, but rather a friendship that will help me in my quest to help society.'

The miseries of the men and women surrounding Florence consumed her thoughts. She hadn't yet discovered her calling, but she was full of plans for the good of her fellow beings, and she had learned to turn to Milnes for understanding, counsel, and assistance.

On that evening, Richard Monckton Milnes confided in Edward MacCarthy, an engineering student friend of his, as they sipped brandy at a small table away from the tipsy crowded service counter and the people's sneezes, coughs, snores, and bad breathy whistles, who were all gathered for the warmth of a smoggy ambience in a tavern in the heart of Hampshire.

'I experience conflicted feelings. Feelings of wanting to be in love yet being unable to.'

'Fame, fame, fame, is distracting you.'

Richard admitted, 'She is very lovely, but I don't know; I can easily get her out of my head.'

'Listen, dear friend, don't dare to make proposals if your feelings are not those of romantic passion. Your romanticism is limited to books and travel; women need your attention. What about your fame, which makes it fortunate for you not to be committed to just one woman? How can you maintain the concentrated attention needed for a wonderful love?' MacCarthy said.

'Oh, come on, the reason is that I'm too busy with commitments—not with ladies, but with writing and charitable work. Yes, I am aware of my fame, and I believe that women naturally gravitate towards prominent men.'

'But Florence is different,' MacCarthy remarked, bending his head backwards and turning the brandy glass towards his lips to make sure not a single drop of brandy was left within. He kept his eyes fixed on the rough wooden beam over his head as he said, 'She wants you to help her in what she has in mind; she is a rare woman, a woman with intellect, and ready to work hard in this world.'

***

Florence's desire to shine in society was growing stronger. She was confident that she could accomplish whatever she believed in. She met other people engaged in charitable work through her connections, and it was at this point that she felt compelled to start supporting them as they helped the sick and the impoverished. From her wealth, she provided food, clothing, and bedding, as well as purchasing medicines. She also paid visits to their impoverished, filthy huts and tried to teach them proper hygiene.

She felt better once she donated her belongings. Her

gloomy mood improved because helped the poor and contributed to them. She would spend hours away from her home visiting houses where people were pleading for help due to their poverty or medical conditions. She went to workhouses, slums, and filthy schools.

God spoke to her once more as she prayed and documented in her journal what she experienced daily with these helpless people. She was on the correct path. She was hurting from her family's criticism of her choices, but the spirit inside her alleviated the pain when she helped the less fortunate, and she realised she was progressing as a result. Florence then received a letter saying that her grandma was in a seriously ill condition and requested that Florence takes care of her. Florence voluntarily agreed, took the grandmother's spare key from her father's desk, and left Embley to reside in the opulent brown brick home that stood out among the other homes in the heart of the village.

The bells rang loudly in the belfry, summoning the believers who were hurrying down the streets to make it to church on time. When Florence observed the widespread poverty most people experienced, a dark aura surrounded her. She finally reached Granny's door after wading through muddy alleyways, passing by street vendors, and rushing hansom cabs. As she turned the door key, she heard a voice wail in agony.

'Oh my God, please help!'

'It's Florence.'

'Oh, Flo, come in, dear; I'm where the living room

used to be,' whimpered Granny from beneath her covers.

'A downstairs bedroom is no sin when your feet give out,' Florence consoled her grandmother while gathering up some of the clothing that had fallen to the ground and putting it back on the chair.

'This fever pain is eating me alive.'

'Would you like a second blanket?'

'No, my dear Flo, my body is definitely at the wrong temperature this morning, but not quite as feverishly as yesterday.'

'This will help the fever go down,' Florence replied, wetting a towel in the washbasin she found hanging by the bedside. 'Lift your head so I can properly wrap it around your neck.'

'I'm truly impressed by your expertise, my dear.'

'I still know nothing. I still have a lot to learn, but what I've already discovered from notes kept by certain doctors and the people I meet and who share their knowledge with me gives me motivation to start helping the sick.'

'I informed the vicar yesterday of your visit and did let him know how much you have improved.'

Florence was about to place another cushion under her grandmother's head when a loud knock on the door was heard. She hurried to check who it was, leaving the cushion on the armchair. When she answered the door, she was met by a terrified man dressed in a fitted dark blue suit who was soaking wet from the torrential rain.

'The vicar sent me here to look for someone named Flo.'

'Oh, come in from the rain; I am Flo.'

'My wife, my wife,' the man said, 'she is so sick, and the vicar said you can help.'

'Give me a moment, please.'

Florence entered Granny's room and filled her grandmother's glass with more water while she set a cushion under her head. 'I have to leave you a bit on your own to assist someone else in the village,' she said. 'The vicar sent a person here for me to go with him.'

'Go, go, my dear, be careful.'

A wave of illness that hit Chawton village seemed to herald the arrival of winter severely. Several other people, in addition to that man's wife, also had fever and discomfort. Florence gave the villagers her entire attention, caring for them and using her knowledge to help them in any way she could. She was aware of other things along her path as she found herself on her own, assisting all of these folks. She knew from personal experience how important it was to have professional medical education and training to properly care for the sick. This was a startling revelation for her, and it would be an even bigger shock to the upper class out there, which was eager to party and have a good time but never really paid attention to serious concerns like this. They continued to believe that nursing entailed being an elderly, coarse lady who was typically stupid, always filthy, wearing bunched-up, squalid clothing, sipping from a brandy bottle, and engaging in other odd behaviours.

Florence felt as though she was being drawn into a future in which she would have to make an effort to change people's perceptions of what a nurse actually does, all the while thinking about her own job, career, and knowledge in order to demonstrate that she was a true model of a nurse. Her profession as a nurse—a real nurse working within a hospital system—had by this point become clearer than it had been before.

That was the pivotal moment in her life, yet saying the words 'nurse' or 'hospital' was risky. How would she explain it to her parents?

Florence was miserable about the state of her family. They made regular travels from Hampshire to London, then to the north for the summer season at Lea Hurst in Matlock, Derbyshire, before returning to Embley once more for their social life and to maintain intimate contacts with significant and dominating individuals, celebrities, dukes, and ambassadors. They would frequently travel to London to mix with the important people of high society. They were entirely uninterested in Florence's future, so they made sure to keep themselves occupied to avoid discussing her plans, which they intended to sweep under the rug in the hopes that Florence would get married and stop thinking about her goals and aspirations.

CHAPTER FOUR

The Darkest Era

1842–1848, Hampshire

In her room alone, Florence Nightingale continued to stab her pen in frustration as she scribbled angry notes about her life, the things she was feeling, and the things she was seeing that disturbed and severely wounded her. Florence recorded the complaints of women who were experiencing mental breakdowns. They were left alone for the entire day to do nothing but relax in a living room, converse, read, and drink tea and coffee. After a day of inactivity, women would end up having mental breakdowns and being enraged at not being permitted to be independent. Was independence among women a sin? Why couldn't women accomplish tasks or work that men could? Were women less capable than men? Did they possess less mental sway?

Florence's high education level, which at the time was reserved for men, caused her much frustration. She aspired to put her theories and knowledge into practice, but to her parents' dismay, she suffered from crippling sadness, hallucinations, and suicidal despair.

All of this did not deter Florence Nightingale; she continued to put her attention on her own education, with a focus on mathematics. Although overcoming mental health challenges required strength and effort, she was able to stay concentrated on her objectives with patience and drive.

She had not yet engaged in the real practice of nursing, but she was now confident that her vocation lay with the sick in hospitals. The next critical step was convincing her parents to send her to Salisbury Infirmary, a few miles from Embley, where she would learn nursing. Florence had already met Dr. Fowler, the chief physician of the Salisbury Infirmary, who was intrigued by her education.

During the Christmas season, the Fowlers, old aristocratic friends of the Nightingales, arrived to stay at Embley for a holiday and were warmly welcomed by Fanny. Florence believed that this was the ideal opportunity to present her idea.

One evening, at the appropriate mealtime, Fanny had everything set perfectly in accordance with the Nightingales guidelines for mealtime conduct, including the seating arrangement, the preparation of the variety of courses, and the etiquette of serving the food. The dining room was warmly decorated for Christmas and had wreaths hanging on the main fireplace.

The appropriate subjects of conversation at the table were also part of the rubric of conduct, until

Florence, who was listening to the conversation of Dr. Richard Fowler, who at Salisbury was experimenting with open-air consumption treatment and remarking on the shortage of personnel working in the infirmary, put down her fork, wiped her lips, and spoke. 'Dr. Fowler, I apologise for interrupting, but you know that my desire is to become a nurse and that you are aware of the knowledge I have already attained.'

'I know you're interested; if you're allowed, you'd be more than welcome.'

A storm erupted at these words. Fanny and Parthe hurled themselves backwards in their chairs after swallowing what was in their mouths. Fanny and Parthe's eyes were filled with terror. Her father looked bewildered at the visitors before turning to look at his wife, who had already pursed her lips and narrowed her eyes to contain her resentment for her daughter.

Then Fanny replied indignantly to Dr. Fowler, 'Don't you think this would be absurd for my daughter to work in a horrific place and in a shameful position?'

'The perception of a drunken nurse must end. I am actively performing the tasks that a nurse should perform; Florence is aware of my advanced perspectives on this profession.'

'I don't care; she's our daughter, and we get to decide what's best for her.'

'But…'

'Sorry, I'm retiring; I'm not feeling well.' They both retired to their rooms after throwing the serviette on the table with wrath and signalling to Parthe to follow her.

The Fowlers could sense the tension in the air, but they kept eating without saying a word. Florence likewise retired to her room later, heartbroken and depressed about the resistance she may now expect from her parents.

Dr. Fowler broke the stillness by telling William Nightingale about his daughter.

'Don't ignore her and do allow her to pursue her aspirations; she is a bright young woman.'

'We know she has great intellect, but we are afraid to send our daughter to a hospital environment. You know better than I what conditions hospitals are in.'

'The hospitals' conditions will improve; they must improve; the unsanitary conditions must end. In addition, hospitals like Kaiserwerth and the Salisbury Infirmary are ahead in this; we boast of cleanliness and safe water supplies.'

William paid close attention to Dr. Fowler as he attempted to comprehend Florence's condition. He cared deeply for his daughter and didn't want her to carry around a wounded heart.

'Just think about it. Imagine being ill and having to go to the hospital; you can't possibly stay at home because you might need surgery.' Dr. Fowler added, 'Wouldn't you be outraged and frantic if you found no clean beds, no clean water, no surgery tables, no proper aid from hospital staff, from a nurse, nothing?'

'Agreed.'

'This is the breakthrough your daughter wants to bring about. Nurses, we doctors need them, but we also need nurses who are knowledgeable on health issues, knowledgeable of what we as doctors are doing in a surgery, knowledgeable of the importance of cleanliness, clean water, sanitation, medication, and psychological assistance to the patient while they are going through their health problems. She aims to shift the public perception of nurses away from the abnormalities they are often linked with.'

'She needs to be trained, though.'

'If you let her go, you will be amazed at her success,' said Dr. Fowler. 'We have given training to some nuns in Rome and at Kaiserswerth; nuns who already had an idea of such health practices as they master them between themselves in the convents, but the number is not enough, and it shouldn't be the work of nuns. Nuns are welcome, but doctors and hospitals really require well-trained nurses. Nurses must be nurses.'

The following day, William tried to put up with Florence Nightingale's sadness while also explaining the situation to Fanny. He made an effort to convince her that what they were doing to their daughter was unfair and that she ought to be allowed the freedom to follow her ambitions.

Fanny vehemently disagreed, saying, 'No, no, and no, I'm not letting my daughter be a wretched nurse; she should be marrying a wealthy high society man and becoming a mother and making us grannies.'

'But we cannot plan for our children; they must decide; they are the steerers, and...'

'And we need to show them the way to go, for their own sake and for our sake, for the sake of our reputation in society. It will be embarrassing for us if she takes that path.'

'But you saw her this morning; she didn't eat anything, and she doesn't even look well.'

'That's because she and her sister had a fight yesterday.'

'I overheard them arguing, but this shouldn't be happening, and it's all our fault.'

'For God's sake, are you blaming ourselves now?'

'We must speak with Flo and then calmly sit down and resolve the issue.'

'She's ruining our lives; I'm not going anywhere today because of her, I don't feel like dancing and laughing, and I won't go anywhere if our friends find out she's going to work in hospitals; what a disgrace, a family disgrace.'

'My poor daughter is always locked in her room, and I don't want to keep seeing her like that. Fanny, I'm asking you to pay attention to what I'm saying because Dr. Fowler is correct in needing Florence in his hospital.'

Fanny snatched her domed, bell-shaped skirt and stormed upstairs as her tears were streaming down her face.

Florence continued to experience this anguish and frustration. She stayed motivated by writing. This was her sole option for transferring her knowledge onto paper. The knowledge she had gleaned from key persons she encountered during her gaiety life, such as politicians, philanthropists, writers, and doctors. Every dinner, every social gathering, and every dance were never a waste of time; rather, they served as opportunities to learn about what was happening in the actual world.

She persevered in pursuing her goals with strength and steadiness. She kept writing letters and talking with contacts she had, and she kept convincing the individuals she knew that her capacity to shine in the community would truly benefit everyone in need.

God's call on her life would not be shattered; she was determined to fulfil it.

CHAPTER FIVE

The Struggle

1848–1850, Hampshire

Florence was once again completely collapsing. She saw herself as an eagle poised to take flight and start a revolution, but the eagle was restrained in an iron cage. Frustrated, in tears, in pain, unable to sleep, and wanting to actually pass away rather than see daybreak. Her vision, ambitions, and targets imprisoned her.

Florence, however, had the strength to hold on to the goals she had set for herself. She still made progress despite clinging to these intense desires. She knew that one day the chains that bound her would shatter and she would be free, so she found the determination to study and seek nursing knowledge.

During a dinner, her father introduced her to the Right Honourable Lord Ashley, a politician, reformer, and philanthropist.

'Your ambitions should not be denied. Your father and I have spoken. It is not an easy chore to deal with sanitation, hospitals, and health.'

'In fact, most of the time I feel lost, bewildered, and

unsure of what to do next. If my parents will let me, I know I need hands-on training, but I also want to read and study.'

'You should read the hospital reports and the Blue Books since they include information about our sanitary and public health issues. I can also provide you with letters from the House of Commons, discussion reports on the City of London's hygienic standards, and information about the state of our insane asylums. Such topics are constantly being discussed.'

'I appreciate your recommendations and will obtain these reports.'

'And as promised, I'll provide you with the letters the House of Commons sent to me so you know what we're talking about.'

She began creating her own reports after studying these and comparing them to the information she had already learned about the state of hospitals from doctors and other philanthropists. Her own journals were filled with statistics, data, analogies, and notes she had already written. Florence was using all of her knowledge to write and draught the foundation for hospital hygienic conditions while working in peace, secrecy, and solitude in her room. Florence was to become the first specialist in Europe in this field.

Florence Nightingale turned thirty on May 12, 1850. She noted, 'This is the age Christ began his mission,' in her notebook. 'No more silly things now. Love is over. No more marriage proposals, please. Now,

Lord, help me to focus entirely on Your will and what You want me to do.'

The Bracebridges, who were close friends with the Nightingales, were made aware of Florence's condition by her mother, Fanny, who voiced their concern for their daughter's wellbeing. As a result, they persuaded Florence's father to let her travel with them for the sake of her mental health. The entire time, Fanny remained silent. She was nearly ready to admit that she was perplexed by her younger daughter's eccentricities.

Florence left Embley to see more of the world. This long journey led her to Egypt. Although she enjoyed the beauty of Egypt's surroundings and knew that there were countless wonders there, her depression made her feel uneasy. She fought psychologically to find peace within herself and be comfortable in the moment. It goes without saying that she took the chance to stop by any charitable institutions she passed. She spent time with the St. Vincent de Paul sisters in Alexandria, in their immaculate schools and the visitors' quarters of their convents. They had to go from Greece to Berlin and Prague on their way back.

Florence's personality was energising and invigorating, despite her sadness and depression. She was getting over her disappointing past. She visited medical facilities and nonprofit organisations while in Berlin. Finally, she arrived in Kaiserswerth.

Kaiserswerth was not only a hospital. Its founder, Theodore Fliedner, who was a theologist, was aware of the social work that was needed in society at that time. He initiated his work administering spiritual and physical needs to prisoners, but Pastor Theodore knew that the wave of the needy was immense.

He welcomed Florence Nightingale and showed her over his buildings, which now comprised the hospital, the day and infant school, the Magdalen asylum, the orphan asylum, the lunatic asylum for women, and the training school, where school mistresses were trained and then sent to teach in schools or become governesses to private families. There was also the parent-house, or house of education, for the two classes of sisters, namely, both the nursing and teaching sisters, during the time that they were going through the various departments, under the direction and supervision of experienced deaconesses. She then put on the distinguishing dress, a blue spotted cotton with a plain linen collar, and a spotted muslin cap.

Florence was brought up as a good housekeeper, a practical foundation that was valuable at Kaiserswerth.

'My dear, are you certain that you are prepared for this difficult work?'

Without giving a verbal reply but as proof of what she was ready to do, Florence grabbed her skirt to lift it up above her knees, and gently kneeling on the floor next to a bucket of water, she rubbed a large wet brush across a bar of soap and began scrubbing the floorboards.

Then Pastor Fliedner bent slightly down and

praised her for the work she had just completed. He said, 'You are a dedicated soul for this profession; you understand that this is not just work but a vocation.'

She smiled and nodded, approving Pastor Fliedner's words. She was delighted, and her excitement was expressed in a letter she drafted from Kaiserswerth to her father. 'The world here fills my life with interest.'

A week later, Florence started to draft the notes in the form of a booklet under the title, '*The Institution of Kaiserswerth on the Rhine for the Practical Training of Deaconesses, under the direction of the Rev. Pastor Fliedner, embracing the support and care of a hospital, infant and industrial schools, and a female penitentiary.*'

Florence's accomplishment didn't last long because Kaiserswerth was not to be mentioned when she got home. Her mother was furious and sobbing uncontrollably, thinking that it was sad and despicable that her daughter had gone to such a place. Parthe became terrified when she realised that her sister, Flo, might lose her place in the family if she failed to perform the customary tasks that were expected of her.

The disputes persisted. Parthe, Florence's sister, had to be cared for because of her outbursts of unreasonableness, senselessness, and outright lunacy. She desired having Florence to herself, caring for her, and engaging in activities with her at home like they did when they were younger. Florence, on the other hand, desired to soar in the world and could not confine herself within four walls.

Months went by. While in her chamber, Florence stomped her foot on the floor. She couldn't afford any more desperation.

'I cannot and will not stay here,' Florence stuttered.

She moved to her tiny desk and wrote a letter to Kaiserswerth with trembling hands. The paper was folded and sealed, and she clutched it firmly, almost wrinkling it.

She ran outside after slamming the bedroom door wide open with her shoulder. She continued to walk with her face hidden under the bonnet, looking down at the ground. She made a beeline for the penny post with no desire to interact with anyone.

Florence didn't take her seat during the evening's meal gathering. Her mother and father exchanged glances while raising an eyebrow. They had been waiting for this time, and it appears that it has finally come. Parthe was slumped backward in her chair, staring at her knees with a glum expression. Florence paced around the serving table.

'I don't expect or want compassion or support from you, but I do want to tell you that I am leaving.'

Her mother pulled the lace serviette that hung at her embroidered neckline and slammed her fist on the table, asking, 'Leaving to where?'

William prompted her to calm down.

'Kaiserswerth, they need me there; the shortcomings in hospitals are huge, and I am ready to perform my duties.'

William and Fanny stared at each other, their eyes wide open, on hearing the word Kaiserswerth.

The atmosphere in the room was one of complete silence. Florence rushed away and sobbed in the garden. Parthe and her parents were still seated at the table, appearing to be at a loss for words. Her father was now focusing his attention on the cutlery. Slowly picking up a fork, William attempted to balance it on his fingertip.

'We need to be in balance with Florence's decisions, just as I'm trying to balance this fork,' William said. 'We must acknowledge that the Herberts and the Bracebridges, two of our charitable, workaholic friends who are already aware of and supportive of her ambitions, are correct and that Florence's intentions are quite honourable.'

'Shameful, shameful; hospitals are shameful,' answered Fanny.

'Yes, they are, but we need to find a balance between what she desires and what we can approve of her desires; otherwise, she will escape,' replied William.

Days passed with no communication between Florence and her parents. Florence was getting ready to travel to Kaiserswerth. While she was writing in her diary, she was disturbed by a gentle knock on her bedroom door.

'Come in,' she said, and her parents did. Florence continued to write.

Fanny seemed miserable and unwell. They sat on Florence's bed, looking at their daughter. William finally broke the stillness.

'We are prepared to travel with you on this journey. You will be accompanied by your mum and Parthe. We don't want our daughter to travel on her own.'

'But please, don't say anything outside Embley. It's a shame, so don't mention anything about where we're going,' Fanny urged, adding, 'We will travel in secrecy, and when the coachmen ask us where we are going, say Duesseldorf.'

Two days later, the coachmen were given the order to begin the voyage and take the women to Duesseldorf via Cologne. With all they said to Florence, Fanny and Parthe made the journey dramatic.

'It's entirely your responsibility,' Fanny said. 'You're making me sick with your decisions.'

Parthe scowled. 'You're a humiliation; weren't you happy living a luxury life?'

Florence remained silent. The best would be for her to not respond. However, Fanny and Parthe crushed Florence's heart with constant expressions of hatred, like those throughout the entire journey. There was a great finale of enmity between the two sisters at the Carlsbad Hotel before Florence left on her own for Kaiserswerth, which was only a mile away.

Parthe glared angrily at the standing mirror in the

hotel room and saw the image of her sister packing the last few things she needed, saying, 'You are stupid; you are keeping to your own desires and have changed our lives in a disastrous way.'

Parthe exasperatedly turned and threw some bracelets in Florence's direction as she was saying, 'Look at papa, he is so upset and can't take it any longer. If anything happens to him, I'll kill you.'

Florence's heart was severely wounded, and she wanted to sit down and cry, but she rose resolutely, gripped her luggage bag, and then disappeared outdoors onto the foggy roads, gesturing to halt a horse coach that would carry her to Kaiserswerth.

CHAPTER SIX

The Work in Hospitals

1850, Germany

The workload at Kaiserswerth was enormous. The hospital deaconesses had to put in countless hours of work. Florence Nightingale felt blessed and in tune with life despite all her work and seldom a moment's rest. She gave it all, and she was eager to learn and gain more knowledge. Florence was present at surgeries as well as working with children and at the hospital. She outlined the shortcomings she came across and offered suggestions on how they might be addressed.

Florence met three young doctors from the University of Edinburgh who were on their apprenticeship training here. She was able to build up a rapport with two of them so she could ask about medical matters. She seized every chance to increase her knowledge. Dr Pisani, a Maltese doctor who graduated from the University of Malta but completed his studies in Edinburgh, was among the young doctors.

Florence and Dr Pisani developed a sympathetic

relationship. Together, they used to visit the patients, which for Florence meant gaining experience and expertise. The two of them would then take a break for some fresh air to relieve the stress of hard work, and Dr Pisani, a young, energetic, and diligent doctor, would encourage Florence to stroll down Kaiserswerth's winding streets with him in the direction of the Rhine River.

'Germany is so lovely; the Rhine sounds better to me than the Nile.'

'Oh, certainly, Germany is undoubtedly a beautiful country. Do you have the bread, please?'

After working so hard that morning, including two procedures, Dr. Salvatore asked Florence if she would get him something to eat.

'Yes, of course, here it is: cheese and salted butter.' Then Florence remarked, 'I was considering asking the committee to put little bells next to each bed to call the nurses; I don't want patients to try to call us out loud, as happened yesterday.'

Dr Pisani concurred, saying, 'It's a good idea, and the operating tables need to be moved into brighter rooms with larger windows, so that, thanks to the natural light, we will see better what we are doing on the patients.'

'Since you brought up the subject of surgeries, what was that inhalation you tried to get the patient to sleep and not feel pain?'

'Ah, that's the new technique; we're testing it on

patients by having them breathe in 'ether frolics,' which makes them painless throughout surgery. This is a novel discovery, but it's expensive, so only aristocrats can afford it.'

'It should be for everyone; I'll bring it up with Pastor Theodore's committee, and I need to also discuss the religious aspect with them. Even though this is a Protestant hospital, Catholics are nonetheless welcome since a patient is a patient regardless of his or her religion.'

Dr Pisani was startled by the changes that Florence had in mind; even if she didn't know enough about medicine, she certainly knew enough about hospital administration. She persuaded the committee to submit her recommendations.

No one had ever demonstrated such full mastery of what she had to learn or passed such a remarkable examination as Florence, according to Pastor Fliedner, who shared this sentiment with Mr. Sidney Herbert, an important visitor to Kaiserwerth. Mr. Sidney Herbert had praised Florence's work in Kaiserswerth as an outstanding achievement in the novel techniques used by a nurse.

Florence spent three months in the Institute for Protestant Deaconesses' training programme because she wanted to work in other hospitals to learn about diverse healthcare systems. Nonetheless, Kaiserswerth was a successful beginning.

Not for her mother and sister, whom she met in the

Duesseldorf hotel where she had left them. They were not interested in hearing anything Florence had to say about Kaiserswerth, as they were waiting for her with everything packed and prepared to load the cases into the carriage.

Her mother reprimanded her, saying, 'Stay distant; you might be carrying a disease. We will climb first in the carriage, so you stay opposite us.'

'I will share with you what I have experienced.'

'No, no, thank you; just shut up; we don't want to hear anything about your hospitals.'

They avoided her, treating her dishonourably and acting as if she had broken the law. Florence remained silent but wasted no time. While on the road, she wrote notes, letters, and a list of suggestions for improvements to the hospital systems. Florence understood that this was only the start of her calling and vocation. She was now wishing to visit more hospitals, preferably larger ones.

When they got home, papa William welcomed them and expressed how much he missed his wife and daughters.

'Be careful; she might be infected in her blood,' Fanny warned William.

However, William ignored what his wife had just said and hugged his daughter instead.

'My dear, I'm delighted with how successful you were, the Herberts wrote to me in a letter. You were brilliant in your duties, and Pastor Fieldner was astounded.'

'Let me explain what happened: the pastor had a committee that had to follow my instructions; everything I recommended to them was an innovation.'

Fanny, who didn't give a damn about her daughter's successes, yelled at the housemaid, 'Up, up with the bags, and to the laundry!'

Following that, the housekeeper led Fanny and Parthe to their individual rooms. She assisted them in unpacking their belongings and showed them to their baths, which were prepared with warm water and fine soap.

Florence stayed with her father, telling him about her experiences in Kaiserswerth.

'You should be proud of yourself,' William added as he sipped some brandy.

Florence responded, 'I am in seventh heaven performing the duties of a deaconess, but I was deeply reprimanded by both my sister and my mother throughout the entire journey.'

'Pardon me, I regret sending them to accompany you; it was a mistake on my part.'

'Oh, papa, how I adore you, and if you do... '

'I know what you were going to say—I won't let them go with you again—so there's no need to tell me that,' her father remarked. 'You must be mature enough to be able to travel on your own; therefore, I will grant you permission to do so. I'll let you go, Flo, but any communication must be limited to just you and me.'

Florence burst into tears as she hugged her father. William, in turn, cuddled his daughter and kissed her on the cheek.

Florence had to stay in Embley for the time being. After visiting Kaiserswerth, she had a tonne of information to record in her notes. While she was at home, Florence had another nursing opportunity. Aunt Mai was ill, and Florence cared for her until she recovered. She aided the destitute in the small village of Hursley, as well as other humanitarian needs.

While visiting numerous philanthropic institutions, Florence met individuals from various social ventures. Friendships were developed between them and Florence, and this resulted in a flood of communication. Through such correspondence, she was able to prepare to begin work at a Catholic hospital, the *Maison de la Providence*, a hospital run by the sisters of charity in Paris.

At the breakfast table one morning, Florence noticed her father devouring his plate of fried eggs with gusto.

'I'll be departing for Paris soon, to the sisters of charity hospital, where they have accepted me.'

'Oh, not again! When are you going to put an end to this pantomime of your hospitals?!' Fanny said with rage.

'You have turned our life into an inferno,' Parthe raged.

'Calm down, calm down. She is speaking to me, and you are not involved this time. She is mature enough to travel alone, and I will be fully responsible for her choice,' her father explained.

***

Florence went to Paris on her own this time. Her decision to leave her family behind was a strong one. She decided to visit Mary Clarke first, pay her a visit, stay with her for a few nights, and share some memories at her salon, where she had previously met notable figures, the majority of whom had now passed away. Mary Clarke was delighted. They kept in touch because of her unwavering passion for Florence. She adored her and was conscious of the invaluable information and connections she had given Florence from her past. Mary Clarke was proud to have played a major role in Florence's success.

Before Florence arrived, she instructed the housemaids to create the cosiest possible ambience in Florence's bedroom by stuffing pillows with feathers and using scented bed linen. A simple writing desk that Mary Clarke knew Florence would adore was positioned under the window, and bath oils were placed next to the bathtub.

'Let us assist you with your suitcase, madam,' said the head of the housemaids to Florence upon arrival at Clarkey's mansion. 'I invite you to have a seat, and Miss

Mary Clarke will be with you shortly. Would you care for a beverage, madam?'

'Oh, sure, certainly, a cup of tea would be lovely,' Florence replied.

'Very good, madam.'

At these remarks, Florence heard squeaking door hinges followed by Mary Clarke's footsteps, which she immediately recognised.

'Oh, my dear Flo, what a blessing!' she said, stretching her arms out to hug Florence and trying to maintain her equilibrium as the spirit of drinking seemed to have taken its habitual ritual that evening, and while the housemaid brought the tea, both ladies were already deep in their conversation of memoirs and celebrity names, plans, and connectedness. The evening evolved into late night, which Mary Clarke seemed to have set aside wholly for Florence, absenting herself from her salon.

The day had finally arrived when Florence would be presented to the Reverend Mother at the Providence House. The life Florence had always imagined was now so becoming a reality. Her performance exceeded expectations. She wrote long letters to the hospital's committee in which she detailed everything that needed to be changed. The hospital's techniques were ineffective, and Florence made it clear to everyone what needed to be changed and improved.

Everyone involved was astounded by her knowledge and made an effort to follow her lead and all of her recommendations. The committee, on the other hand, was a complete failure in terms of overseeing and controlling the things she suggested. Florence was stern and to the point in her work, but the committee failed to implement the changes.

Florence assumed leadership of the committee. She performed her nursing duties with commitment, but she was also aware that the hospital needed efficient inventory and financial administration. Without these two pillars, a healthcare system would fail. She needed help from people who were ready to act and not procrastinate.

Long days of work followed, and in Florence, cheerfulness, high spirits, and enthusiasm remained. She was excited about her career, eager to give it her all, and she was making a difference. She felt obligated to write every detail to Mary Clarke. So, in the middle of the night, Florence sat at her tiny workstation in the hospital's storeroom, surrounded by blankets, cushions, bandages, basins, and whatever else was available. She could write letters with the help of the faint light from the oil lamp, beginning, 'To dear Miss Mary Clarke, the work this morning began by assisting in the operating theatre with an amputation...' Florence found that writing and explaining helped her unwind and mentally rewind the entire day. If she had unintentionally forgotten to complete a task because of everyone's constant interruptions, she would jot it down on a piece of paper and tuck it in her pocket to ensure that she would attend to it when the time came. She was active day and night and slept little and only for brief periods, but the vigour and excitement she felt inside gave her more energy than she needed. Every minute, a stream of people needed aid.

'If there is no arrowroot available today for him, could you perhaps suggest something to help his stomach?'

'Please provide more bandages for the surgery patient.'

'Mr. Gaffi wants to question you regarding the orders you have drafted.'

'There is a food delivery at the door.'

Such was Florence's hectic schedule. The hospitals were a really difficult nut to crack. The problems were not just with the patients but also with the hospital infrastructure.

'Sewage is leaking down the side path of the main entry; present systems are not keeping up.'

'We need to put in a mechanised hoisting system from this floor to the other; it will make carrying patients, equipment, and supplies much easier.'

Similar difficulties and setbacks were common. Florence didn't let any of these difficulties break her spirit—everything was still in its early stages. She was getting stronger. Her management of the hospital was excellent. She oversaw all levels of staff, from storekeepers to nurses and administrators.

'I should give orders to you to remove those items

from the stores because I need to know and record what went out.'

'Food should be given to the patient as directed by the doctor, and I need to know so that I can keep records.'

'I need to show you how I keep the statistics; they're crucial so we can see how the hospital's systems work.'

Everyone appreciated the effectiveness of Florence's systems. She was able to incorporate the nurses and patients into a system of keeping records, following advice, respecting doctors' orders, and following a set of processes for everything that was done.

Fame soon grew; other notable people took note of Florence's recognition. Even when she received an invitation to a party from a well-known person, she still made time to go. At every event she attended, she was greeted as the dearest of all, and she was admired more than ever.

The letters of gratitude, affection, and thanks she received from her patients revealed her idiosyncrasies in hospital management and the job she achieved among the patients, as well as her charisma and indulgence.

Florence provided medical as well as spiritual care for her patients. She was able to relate to them, share in their emotions, and support them even when they needed money.

Florence was getting letters from all over. Patients, nurses, and medical professionals from other hospitals wrote to her, requesting more matrons to help in their facilities.

She set out on her own, visiting various institutions and gathering information to develop an innovative approach for treating the issues she had identified. The Herberts kept in touch with her since they were also in charge of hospitals and the reform was complex and challenging to understand. Corruption, nepotism, and bribery must all be eradicated in hospitals. Nursing education was in its early stages.

Cholera broke out in London during the summer of 1854, and hospitals were overcrowded. Several nurses died as a result of the illness, while others ran away. Day and night, Florence was there, going between wards and assisting patients while constantly on her feet. Behind the outer appearance of a charming, sweet, and kind lady, there was a lady of steel.

However, a more significant catastrophe in the outside world was developing into a global crisis. England and France, the allies, waged war on Russia and invaded the Crimea. The importance of hospitals has increased dramatically.

CHAPTER SEVEN

The War Outbreak

1853, Scutari

In Scutari, the British forces established three hospitals: The General Hospital, The Barracks Hospital, and The Stable Hospital.

Despite the fact that the hospitals were built to help the allied forces, a cholera outbreak was what brought about tragedy and inefficiency rather than the war's influx of fatalities. The hospital was overflowing with cholera cases, and thousands of sicker and more injured people were crossing the Black Sea to get to Scutari. The traumatic journey was undertaken on ships. These vessels weren't very special; they were just referred to as 'sailing hospitals' because they contained some medication and medical supplies. Nonetheless, these ships were an absolute mess. They had to transport thousands of victims across the Black Sea at once, even though they were only intended to take a few hundred. Everyone was falling on top of one another in filth, crammed like sardines, and too weak to reach sanitary facilities.

When the injured arrived at the hospital, they were given next to nothing. There weren't enough doctors to attend to everyone; beds were full; new casualties had to be left lying on the floor; there weren't enough cups or buckets to share water among patients; there weren't enough operating tables, chairs, blankets, or linen for bandages; and there weren't enough food or supplies to provide food for the patients.

William Howard Russell, a reporter assigned to cover the Crimean War, broke the news of this calamity in The *Times*. England was astonished to learn about all these British Army failings while still being in the dark about what was happening. He explained the anguish that the injured soldiers were going through and how there were no physicians or medical supplies available; the news had come out of nowhere. According to Russell, the French Army had better health care provisions than the British Army.

The news item made it to Mr. Herbert's desk, who had recently been appointed Secretary of War and was in charge of caring for the injured and ill. In light of the fact that he was to blame and that Countess Catherine Woronzow, a Russian noblewoman, was his mother, controversy quickly arose. The political sensitivity of Mr. Herbert's position was evident. He immediately took action by writing to the British Ambassador in Turkey to request that he provide everything necessary to the British Army Hospital at Scutari.

Additionally, he got in touch with Malta, a nearby British-ruled nation, to let the governor, Sir William Reid, know that the Crimea urgently required medical professionals. He wrote a lengthy letter to Florence Nightingale, advising her to organise a nursing brigade to aid in Scutari.

In response to Mr. Herbert's letter, Florence wrote, 'I read about the situation and have already acted; I am taking with me forty nurses, and we will be sailing to Turkey in three days.'

In a second letter to Florence, Mr. Herbert verified what constraints Florence would experience, listed the medical supplies that the British ambassador to Turkey had already delivered to Scutari Hospital, and indicated that numerous surgeons had already left for Constantinople. Mr. Herbert wrote, 'You are no longer just ladies who have no idea what a hospital is. You are now knowledgeable and ready to be hands-on, offering all types of assistance required.'

Also in this letter, Mr. Herbert delegated to Florence the responsibility and task of supervising and leading the team and the scheme at Scutari. 'I only know one person who is qualified to carry out this task, and that person is YOU.'

CHAPTER EIGHT

The Voyage

1854, Marseilles

The group departed London Bridge early on October 21, 1854, to sail via Boulogne Harbour, on the French coast opposite Britain. The sight of Florence Nightingale and the nurses delighted the Boulogne residents. They offered them provisions of food as well as their best wishes for success on their mission while waving their kerchiefs. The journey continued towards Paris, where Florence Nightingale needed to purchase a warehouse full of various provisions and goods. The shipment was to be loaded onto the ship *Vectis*, which was to be waiting at the port for the voyage from Marseilles to Constantinople. Then, a ferry would depart from Constantinople and go over the Sea of Marmara to the Barrack Hospital in Scutari, which was located two hundred and ninety-nine miles from Sebastopol and Balaclava in the Crimea and across the Black Sea. The *Vectis* was a converted postal ship that was already regarded at the time as being unseaworthy. It was a steam-powered ship that transported mail from Marseilles to Malta. The ship was plagued with cockroaches and mice.

The sea journey began, and the vessel encountered strong seas. The ship was violently battered by the waves as it started to rock side to side, and almost all of the sails were torn by the strong winds. Rain that looked like glass needles fell in torrents on the deck. Due to the severe storm, the majority of the load, including guns and other ordnance, had to be abandoned because keeping it would have put them at risk of sinking. Everyone on board was seasick. By hook or by crook, the ship eventually docked in Maltese ports.

The Maltese understood everything there was to know about the Crimean War. Local media covered every development when the conflict broke out in March 1854. Malta was then acting as a military base for the troops' training before they were dispatched to the front in the Crimea. This small island in the middle of the Mediterranean served as a storage facility for food and ammunition, a maintenance facility, and a base for the military hospital thanks to its strategic location on the map. On this island, labour was in full swing.

Ships arriving daily carrying troops and supplies like tools and wood into the Maltese island's harbours kept the port areas busy. Bomb shells were being produced at the Malta Naval Dockyard for use in sinking the Russian fleet.

May 1854 marked the beginning of the war's two-month intensification, during which time the number of injured and killed increased. The Governor of Malta, Sir William Reid, gave the Admiral Superintendent of Malta permission to ask the local medical staff for assistance, and swift action was taken.

Four prominent Maltese doctors volunteered their services and boarded the H.M. screw propulsion ship *Algiers* bound for the Crimean Peninsula. On board the steam corvette *Fury,* another Maltese physician departed for the same location. They were meant to aid the wounded on the Crimean battlefields.

Florence Nightingale, along with other nurses and nuns, experienced severe seasickness upon arriving in Malta on October 29, 1854. Florence lay on her straw bed for nearly a day, vomiting and feeling woozy. It was difficult for her to stand. Thanking God that they arrived safely on the island, those who felt good desired some fresh air and a walk around, so they disembarked the vessel.

The Maltese were curious when they saw a group of women marching up towards the city. Maltese touts approached them, offering to convey them in carts or carriages.

'Carry a lady best, Madam?' was the typical ride-selling phrase in poor English.

'No, thank you; we prefer to walk,' prompted the nurses and nuns.

Meanwhile, in response to Mr. Herbert's final letter, Sir William Reid suggested that Dr Pisani, another exceptional young Maltese physician, would help Florence in her work at Scutari Hospital.

Dr Pisani eagerly accepted. He considered it a privilege to work alongside Florence Nightingale. Dr Pisani rode in his horse-drawn carriage to the docks on the day the ship *Vectis,* carrying Florence Nightingale and her staff of nurses, moored.

Dr Pisani approached the ship and asked permission to board; this was immediately granted. He moved slowly down the underdeck, allowing his eyes to adjust to the darkness before proceeding. The blackness below deck was in sharp contrast to the sun's glittering rays on the deck. He accelerated his pace as he approached the rooms where he could hear groaning sounds of agony.

He tapped on one of the rooms' doors, and a faint voice said, 'Come in.'

'I am a doctor; do you desire any assistance?'

'Oh, come in, come in,' answered Florence, this time with a slightly steadier voice.

'Good morning, I am Dr…' He felt his tongue being swallowed so he wouldn't have to introduce himself when he didn't have to. From Kaiserswerth, he already knew Florence, and he was happy to see her again.

'What a coincidence to have entered this harbour; Sir William Reid summoned me to assist you at Scutari, but I never expected you to be here in Malta,' Dr Pisani remarked, still standing at the doorway.

Florence said as she struggled to lift her head off the cushion, 'Oh, Dr Pisani, we really need help here.'

Dr Pisani hurried over to her side, kneeling, and

placing another pillow beneath her head. Then he opened his case and brought out the stethoscope. 'Madame, please allow me to check your abdomen and listen to your heartbeat.'

Florence raised her skirt just a bit so that he could inspect her medically. He first listened to her heartbeat, then to her abdomen. Without saying a word, he reached into his leather bag and withdrew a black glass bottle.

'For the time being, you must swig a small amount of this medication. It will alleviate your seasickness,' said the doctor.

In an effort to take the medicine straight from the bottle, Florence tried to lift her head a little bit. She then scowled. The taste was unpleasant.

'I know, I know,' said Dr Pisani, 'try to sip a bit more.'

'It tastes like ginger spice,' replied Florence.

'You nailed it; in fact, it is made of ginger; it will lessen your motion sickness.'

'It was my greatest honour to help you,' Dr Pisani said, gazing at Florence's face, which was beginning to pink a little.

The voluntary medical aid provided by Dr Pisani on board was greatly appreciated by Florence. He checked each nurse, nun, and other passenger who was exhibiting essentially the same symptoms. Then he returned to Florence's cabin.

'I have no words to thank you, Dr Pisani,' said Florence.

'It's a great honour to assist you all,' replied Dr Pisani.

'We need you on board here as we still have another five days rolling on this terrifying and distressing sea.'

'I accepted and confirmed with Sir Reid; I've sent him a note with my messenger that I will be in Scutari with you,' Dr Pisani responded. He then hurriedly stamped his feet three times to kill a few crimson bugs before slipping back between the planks.

'Oh, I really appreciate your help, doctor,' Florence said, her face now beaming. She then paused, glanced up at the filthy planks above her head, and added, 'How I wish to get out for a while before we leave for Constantinople.'

'Shall we? I'll help you if you want.'

Holding the doctor's hand, Florence forced a slight grin while attempting to get up from a sitting position.

'Yeah, that's better; I am not used to lying down for so long.'

'Do rest your body on me as I hold you tightly; don't worry, we'll move cautiously onto the deck.'

Florence stood up on her still-shaky feet and tried to take a few steps while holding onto the doctor's dark grey jacket. Dr Pisani managed to get her on deck despite nearly falling twice.

'Doctor. Sir, your luggage is here,' uttered a sailor on deck, 'where do you desire I put them for you?'

'You can put his luggage in my room,' replied

Florence hastily to the sailor, who nodded and made his way to Florence's room. Then, looking at the doctor, she said, 'I will arrange a room for you as soon as we are out to sea.'

'Oh, thank you… How are you feeling now?'

'I'm still a bit dizzy but much better than an hour ago,' Florence replied, looking around to take in her surroundings and leaning her body against a huge mast. 'Nice historical harbour here; it is the most fascinating harbour I have ever seen. I like those curious little houses with flat roofs up that hill behind those warehouses and their green-painted bay windows,' said Florence while indicating with her forefinger where she was looking.

'Those bay windows, we call them *gallarija*,' replied Dr Pisani, 'the locals spend their time there sitting and staring out at the sea, gawking at passersby and anyone coming into port.'

Leaving Florence sitting near the mast, Dr Pisani paced around the deck looking at the fortifications' scene of all the three cities surrounding the harbour, then he came again near Florence and sat down on a stack of rigging.

'The fortifications of these three cities are spectacular and known to have defended our country,' explained Dr Pisani, then he added, 'each and every stone slab has a story to tell.'

'Absolutely,' said Florence, then she added, 'Here

they come,' pointing her finger to the nurses and nuns marching down the street towards the harbour.

The group was returning to the ship, and the sailors were all busy with their responsibilities as they prepared to sail away. A messenger rushed on board, asking for Florence. He was holding a tiny note in his hand.

Florence waved her hand in the man's direction to let him know she was there. It was from the Governor, Sir William Reid, who offered the assistance of five Maltese men to help her in Scutari with a variety of tasks.

CHAPTER NINE

The Vectis Tough Voyage

1854, Constantinople

The paddles were activated to begin the voyage ahead, with the engines pumping full steam as the *Vectis* was manoeuvred out of the Maltese Grand Harbour. The more it sailed out, the more violently the wind and waves crashed against the wooden hull. The waves were shrieking and creaking on the wood and squeaking boards as the darkness approached.

The *Vectis* was registered for the Peninsular and Oriental Steam Navigation Company at a cost of £52,325. She was built by John and Robert Wight at Cowes, Isle of Wight, to replace an earlier vessel of the same name (taken from the Latin for the Isle of Wight). The *Vectis* was designed for the Marseilles/Malta contract; she and her sister *Valetta* (built by CJ Mare on the Thames) were given paddles rather than screw propulsion because of the speeds required. The *Vectis* had her builders' patent diagonal planking. Her maiden voyage to Marseilles, Malta, and back to Marseilles took mail for Malta.

The ship was only one year old and had already been declared not seaworthy as the oscillating steam engines powered and installed by the renowned T. Penn & Sons were far too big and powerful for the size of the ship.

There were torrential downpours. The one room that had been left empty and designated for Dr Pisani was now filled by the five Maltese men who had joined this mission, so Florence walked back to her room and made an attempt to organise it and clear some space so she could set up a bed and a private place for him. As the current got more powerful and challenging to manage, the contents of the rooms began to rock back and forth. It was all really unsettling. Eating was impossible.

Dr Pisani returned to Florence's room feeling dizzy as well. After medicating practically everyone on board, he was now required to assist and make an effort to maintain himself. She just set out a hay mattress for him, and he felt a gentle hand gliding down his shoulder and helping him sit down.

'Cast aside your anxieties, or *Sans Souci* in French, and let us focus on our goals and what we will achieve,' said Nightingale, praying that this arduous journey would end safely.

After two days, the ship was sailing towards the Myrtoan Sea passage that connects Greece and Crete. One of the harshest winters in a hundred years in the

Mediterranean Sea had to have occurred during this expedition. Everyone was terrified to death as they felt the ship tilt to one side. Heavy items on board were sliding upon sailors, and people were being crushed and suffering serious injuries as a result of the sudden vortex generated by the stormy wind. There were enormous, uncontrollable powers of nature. It was a sheer miracle that they escaped a shipwreck on one of the numerous islands in the Aegean Sea. It was a relief to reach the Sea of Marmara and be closer to Scutari. Since this is an inland section of the sea and a gateway to the Black Sea, the sea's force was milder. The *Vectis* had to dock in Constantinople, and a small ferry had to be taken from there to Scutari.

After nine days of terrible weather and storms, the *Vectis* anchored at Seraglio Point in Constantinople on November 3, 1854. Scutari and the massive Barrack Hospital were visible on the other side of the shore. Florence sat on the ship's deck and calmly admired the stunning surroundings. The Barrack Hospital's enormous, golden quadrangle, which had square towers at each corner, was perched on a hill with views of 'the bright waters of the Bosphorus,' the Sea of Marmora, the Princes' Island, and the scene of Constantinople with its castellated walls, marble palaces, and domes. High Scutari, the 'silver city' that the Turks adored, was nearby.

On November 4, at first light, Lord Stratford, the British ambassador to Constantinople, dispatched Lord

Napier, the embassy's secretary, across the gloomy Bosphorus to greet Florence.

'Row faster, row faster!' Lord Napier shouted to the men rowing his long wooden gondola as it approached the *Vectis*. The passage was challenging because the sea was still turbulent, and the winds were blowing in the opposite direction. Lord Napier disliked sea travel. He preferred more ground stability and to sit at his desk, executing the colonial administration tasks entrusted to him.

The gondola approached the *Vectis*, rumbling the waves against the hull, and while gripping the climbing ropes to reach the deck, Lord Napier peered at the other barques arriving to transport everyone to shore and to unload.

'Good morning and welcome,' said Lord Napier to Florence, who was exhaustedly seated on a wet wooden bench near the stern of the deck.

'My pleasure.'

'Lord Stratford sent me here to escort you on shore and assist you with the unloading.'

'Go ahead, gather your bags, nurses, and let's begin leaving this ship,' commanded Florence.

'Be careful, ladies; the planks are slick, and the wind is twisting and tying the rope ladders together. Maintain your grip tight,' advised Lord Stratford to all on board.

Florence and all the nurses were helped aboard Lord Napier's boats and rowed across to Scutari with the help of the sailors and Dr Pisani. The downpour persisted. The steep slopes to Barrack Hospital were a sea of muck when you arrived on the Scutari shore; there was no road, only an abandoned trail. It was a dramatic scenario. Along the way, there were rats feasting on dead animals. A mass of dead people stitched up in canvas lay on the ground, waiting for the orderlies to transport them away. Some soldiers were tattered and hobbling, assisting each other in whatever way they could to get to the hospital.

A bitter wind blew across the nurses' faces as they waited for Florence and Dr Pisani to unload their gondola. Without saying a word, they all exchanged weary glances with one another, yet their eyes conveyed strength and bravery to everyone there.

CHAPTER TEN

The Barracks

1854–1855, Scutari

The Scutari Hospital building was a hollow square with seven- storey towers at each corner. The central courtyard, which originally served as a large parade ground during the reign of Sultan Abdulmecid I, was now a sea of mud, littered with refuse and amputated arms and legs that had been tossed out of the operating room's window. Within the barracks were a depot for troops, a canteen full of spirits, and a stable for horses. In the gloomy, raucous, filthy, humid air dungeons located deep within the cellars of this fortress, over two hundred women drank, starved, gave birth to children, traded prostitution, and eventually died of cholera. Kilometres of echoing hallways with cracked tile floors and walls that streamed wetness, emptiness, and dullness stretched between each tower and throughout the three storeys of these barracks. On each floor and for miles, beds were piled one on top of the other. The doctors who were already working at Scutari did not receive the appointment of Florence and her nurses well and said among themselves,

'Is this not another government blunder?' inquired a medical professional.

'This is a questionable move; why send a group of women here?' another surgeon said.

'What's wrong with Florence's position when it is official here and authorised by the House of Commons? My opinion is that they are competent.'

'If they knew what they were doing, they could have sent more doctors; doctors are knowledgeable, not nurses.'

'I disagree with you,' Dr Pisani said. 'They are all knowledgeable under Florence's tutelage; I know what I'm saying; I worked with her earlier at Kaiserswerth, and she should be trusted.'

However, after being understaffed and overworked for so long, it appeared to be the final straw for assistance. Also, knowing that Florence had powerful backing from Sidney Herbert and half of the Cabinet, they had no choice but to submit, and having brought another doctor with her; Dr Pisani was a blessing. The lodgings for Florence and her group were not at all comfortable. Ten nuns and fourteen nurses had to share one empty room to sleep. There were no other options other than the kitchen, where two chefs were forced to sleep, and a nearby room that they wanted to occupy but that was still occupied by some amputated parts from the soldiers' bodies before they were dumped in the sea. Every room was disgusting.

There was a severe lack of everything. Asking for things was pointless. Not even the bare basics of life were there, such as furniture, cleaning materials, medical equipment, or an operating table. Everyone had to wash their hands, eat, and drink from their own little tin basin, including the nuns, nurses, and doctors. They had to be ready for any food and water shortages. Due to a lack of candles and lamps, they had to retire to bed in total darkness. Rats and fleas were active throughout the rooms. This hospital situation was a health scandal.

The first action taken by Nightingale was to make the hospital clean and provide necessities. She had enough supplies from Marseilles to get started, but she would soon require more.

'Get the brooms, scrubs, lime, and soap that we brought with us; they are still in their boxes labelled 'cleaning' and try to get the buckets too; they are on the other side of the room,' ordered Florence to some of the nurses as she tried to figure out how she was going to get some water for cleaning since the hospital's water system was completely ineffective.

'We need to get water, clean water,' she said to one of the labourers.

'No clean water here; it's all dirty; the sewers have contaminated it.'

'Oh God, please provide me with water,' Florence prayed to herself.

'I will get you water from my house, Florence, clean water from my well,' replied another labourer, grabbing all the buckets that the other nurses had just brought him. 'You all come with me; all of you, we need to carry a lot of water,' said the labourer to his other mates.

The buckets were returned filled to the brim with clean water, and the nurses rolled up their sleeves and began scrubbing the floors and walls.

Florence was meant to work independently, and the nurses and she would only assist the doctors when they specifically requested it. Only one physician, Dr Pisani, who collaborated closely with Florence and her team, was treating Florence differently.

'Could you please supply more bandages for this soldier's amputation?' begged Dr Pisani to Florence.

'Sure,' Florence said as she handed the bandages to Dr Pisani and prepared to depart.

'No, no, don't go, you go ahead, do the bandaging yourself, I have to help another patient, and as soon as you finish, come looking for me because I need to give you a list of medications to be distributed to the patients,' the doctor said.

Dr Pisani didn't want Florence to submit to the authority of the doctors. He would give Florence unsupervised tasks that didn't require the doctors' immediate attention, such as sorting the medication for the casualties in accordance with their doctors' instructions, changing patients' bandages as needed, watching the preparation of food for specific patients, and other similar jobs.

All of this gave Florence more confidence in the tasks she was carrying out, and the physicians began to give her more responsibility.

With the supplies they had provided, Florence and her group of nuns and nurses assumed leadership. Florence ordered them to carefully organise the stock taking by sorting all the linen, making bandages, and counting the food provision packets. Floors, clothing, and bed linens were constantly being cleaned and washed.

'Cooking needs to be done correctly in accordance with the suitable diet ordered by the doctors,' Florence was instructing her nurses, 'a healthy diet equals good health.'

Florence began teaching the nurses how to cook as well. She had come from Marseilles with arrowroot, wine, beef essences, and portable burners. The injured were given pails of hot arrowroot and port wine, and her team was now in charge of running the kitchen and preparing meals for both the employees and the casualties. However, she followed the official protocol as a nurse, which prohibited giving the patient food or medication unless the doctor gave his or her approval.

'You see, Florence and her nurses are brilliantly assisting me,' Dr Pisani stated to another surgeon.

'Indeed, they have had a significant impact. Both Florence and her nurses have received quality training.'

'Florence is outstanding. She performs fracture and wound dressings more expertly than any other surgeon.'

'And did you notice? She has spread that motherly feeling among the casualties. They confide in her and trust her to write them letters and listen to their concerns.'

'Because she is a woman.'

'Haven't you seen what a habit these soldiers now have?'

'They kiss her shadow,' Dr Pisani remarked. 'Florence's quick action in treating one of our soldiers' injuries prevented his arm from being amputated. As Florence walks by his bed, the soldier kisses Florence's shadow with the saved arm. Each soldier is now kissing her shadow.'

One of the troops, overhearing Dr Pisani's chat with the other surgeon, said, 'She is an idol for all of us.' 'If she is speaking to me and the soldier next to me, she nods and smiles to many more at the same time, but she couldn't do it for all, you know, we are hundreds here, but hearing just her voice even from a distance, we lay our heads on the pillow content,' the soldier added.

The second soldier, who was also listening, remarked, 'Before she came, there was such cussing and swearing, and after that, here it is now as holy as a church.'

Florence would sit down in her room every Friday night to take notes, make comments, update store records, reorder supplies, update army statistics, and so on. She hardly had time to lay down on her mattress and relax. And if she had any, troops would see Florence approaching with a faint oil lamp to check on the men who were in severe condition or to give them any medication that the physicians had approved.

CHAPTER ELEVEN

An Influx of Casualties

1855, the Crimea

The Sevastopol battleground quickly transformed into a frozen landscape. They had nothing left to burn, and the layers of clothing they had on were insufficient to keep them warm. Hypothermia prevailed. Amid filth and decaying corpses, the victims—injured and frozen soldiers—poured down to the dock to wait for ships to take them across the Black Sea to Scutari Hospital outside of Constantinople. It was alleged that many wounded soldiers who were enroute on that journey passed away. The travel was rudimentary. Under the supervision of one surgeon, the men dozed on bare decks with just their own jackets covering them. Hell on earth for the soldiers, with blood spattered across the planks, cries of anguish from the unbearable pain, and soldiers drowning after falling overboard.

At Scutari, the sick kept pouring in until the massive stronghold was completely occupied. The supply of straw-filled bags had run out, leaving the wards packed to capacity and the halls crowded with men sprawled on the floor. Disorder ruled. The doctors could not even attend to each patient due to a lack of doctors, nurses, materials, and other services. Even though the doctors and nurses worked nonstop on their feet, the problem persisted beneath the framework of the building. The absence of sanitation was in full force. The infrastructure failed, causing the liquid sludge in the sewers to overflow into the wards. Overcrowding, open wounds, infections, poor ventilation, sanitary failure, and a lack of space all contributed to the shocking death rate. The circumstances were tense. In the Barrack Hospital in Scutari, there were times and locations where even the strongest hand would tremble and the bravest eye would avert its eyes.

Florence continued to update the authorities on the situation at Scutari through her regular letters. Full-time debates were taking place in the House of Commons. The first sanitary commission team was dispatched to see for themselves the flaws that were killing the casualties because Florence had provided them with a clear image of the situation in the hospitals up to the burial sites. The House of Commons recognised in March 1855 that, following this thorough report from Constantinople, prompt action needed to be taken.

Drs Sutherland and Gavin and Mr Rawlinson, to Brigadier-General Lord,
 William Paulet.

Hotel de l'Angleterre, Constantinople, My Lord, 10 March 1855.

The Sanitary Commissioners appointed by Her Majesty's Government to proceed to Constantinople and the Crimea, having inspected the hospital establishments at Scutari, with special reference to their sanitary condition, as referred to in their instructions, have the honour to state to your Lordship,

That we are of the opinion the Barrack Hospital occupies a naturally healthy situation, but that, at no great distance from its walls, there are accumulations of filth which, no doubt, affect the purity of the surrounding air. The wards of the Barrack Hospital are lofty and not overcrowded, but the ventilation is defective and the false floors and box seats in many of the buildings tend to the collection of foul air and other impurities under the woodwork. Had there been time to have prepared the barracks for the purposes of a hospital, this woodwork might have been removed with advantage; but as the building is in use, the defect may, in some measure, be remedied by scrupulous attention to ventilation and cleanliness. One special reason for the defective state of the former is the want of a thorough draught, the ward windows being all on one side.

From the pressure of circumstances, it has been found necessary to make use of the corridors for the reception of the sick. These latter contain much more window space than the wards, and the windows themselves are also loftier. The ventilation of the corridors, therefore, though defective, is better than that of the wards. The most prominent evil connected with these corridors is the condition of the privies, which give out offensive exhalations, despite the evident care bestowed on their cleansing. In several of the wards and corridors, the walls are not as clean as might be desired; in many of the former, the flooring is defective and open, whilst that of the corridors consists mainly of unglazed tile, perhaps one of the worst substances that can be used in a hospital, because of its tendency to absorb moisture and retain excretory fluids. At the time of our inspection, most of the corridors contained two rows of beds; considering the state of the ventilation, we are of the opinion that not more than one row of beds should be permitted.

The water at present supplied to the Barrack Hospital contains organic matter, most of which could be easily removed by filtration.

At the time of our inspection, a considerable portion of the surface of the barrack square was in so moist a state, as to act injuriously on the purity of the air.

Speaking generally, we have great pleasure in expressing our opinion that the Barrack Hospital bears marks of much having been done to improve its sanitary condition; and if the remedies to be hereafter enumerated are applied, everything will have been done that can practically be affected.

The General Hospital—This is the best of all the Scutari hospitals, as its structure admits of adequate ventilation, and the greater part of it is scrupulously clean; besides which, there is nothing except the burial ground (to be afterwards described) likely to affect the purity of the air. Within the court of the hospital, the only point to be noticed is the damp and uneven state of that part of the area used as a thoroughfare.

The most obvious objection to the internal arrangement of the General Hospital is the structure of the privies, from which offensive exhalations proceed. The floor of the kitchen appears to be undrained, for, at the time of our inspection, a considerable quantity of water, capable of easy removal, lay upon it.

The Palace Hospital, Scutari—This establishment occupies a low undrained site, part of which is a marsh, with water lying on the surface. This hospital consists of several buildings, differing in their respective sanitary conditions. The best portions are the theatre and ballroom, which are large lofty apartments, having but one defect, that of ventilation.

The privies attached to this part of the hospital are placed over a running stream, and so far, afford the best instance of an arrangement it is desirable to imitate in the other hospitals when practicable; but at the time of our inspection, offensive exhalations arose from these privies, in consequence of some temporary obstruction.

The remaining portions of the Palace Hospital consist of wards by no means so well suited for their intended purpose. Want of ventilation is here also the main defect, but there is decided overcrowding, and the privy accommodation is extremely bad, the foul exhalations therefrom being sufficient to taint the air for a considerable distance.

The Stable Hospital, Scutari—This hospital consists of four wards over the stables built in the hollow between the Barrack and the General Hospitals. The situation is a bad one, and the relative position of the wards and stables, besides the generally foul condition of the place itself, renders it, in our opinion, quite unfit for the reception of the sick.

Proposed Remedies — To remedy the foregoing defects, we have to request your Lordship to give directions that the following means be at once adopted:

That adequate space for ventilation be provided where necessary, at or as near to the ceiling of each ward as practicable; that, where possible, staircases be made use of as ventilating shafts (for which purpose the partitions between them and the corridors might be rearranged, so as to allow of a free current of air); and that, in all cases, the amount of space for each inmate, exclusive of ventilating shafts and window recesses, be not less than one thousand cubic feet.

That the upper portions of the windows be, in all cases, opened, and the current of air modified by the insertion of perforated zinc plates, louvre-boarding, or otherwise.

That any of the wards that are not quite clean be at once lime-washed, and that lime-wash be practiced at intervals throughout all the wards.

That lavatories for the use of the sick be provided throughout the hospital, easily accessible from the wards, but in all cases, completely detached from the privies.

That the excreta of the patients be instantly removed from within the walls of the hospitals.

That the outfall sewer of the Barrack Hospital be extended, and a trap placed over its mouth to prevent the wind from acting on its contents and carrying the foul odours into the hospital.

That three openings for ventilation be made in the main sewer between the Barrack Hospital and the outfall, and a wooden tank (to be filled when requisite) placed over the sewer, close to the outer wall of the building, a water- trap being made on the barrack side of the ventilator, and a manhole for cleansing formed over the trap.

That some special means of ventilation be applied to the sheds now in course of erection in the Barrack Square; that flushing tanks be provided for the new privies, and an improvement made in the inclination of the drain leading from them into the main sewer.

That the portions of the Barrack Square now unpaved be formed and coated with stone or gravel.

That the open ditch running from the Stable Hospital through the low ground to the east of the Barrack Hospital, be covered over as far as its point of the outfall.

That the main sewer at the General Hospital be extended, with similar appliances for external ventilation, and for flushing, when necessary, as those recommended for the Barrack Hospital.

That an immediate improvement be made in the privies in the wings of the General Hospital, by removing the upper window sashes, which at present do not open, and by connecting them with the drain running along the west front by means of two short drains, and thus obviating the necessity for the former passing under the hospital at all.

That the surface of the inner court now used as a thoroughfare be formed and coated with stone or gravel.

That the low marshy ground near the Palace Hospital be at once thoroughly drained and the privy accommodation improved, either by flushing through the drains, or, if that be not practicable in this case, that movable boxes be provided in the privies, and their contents frequently removed.

That the closed gallery between the ballroom and theatre at the Palace Hospital be disused and no more patients admitted, as it is unfit for their reception.

That the privies, the sewers, and the drains at all the hospital establishments be thoroughly cleansed, and their contents deodorised and removed.

That peat charcoal be freely used as a deodoriser in the privies, as well as in the removal of all offensive matter.

That the surface of the ground in the vicinity of all the hospital establishments be regularly cleansed at short intervals.

That the water tanks be examined and cleansed when necessary, and that the water be filtered in future.

That the removal of all offensive matter and the

general cleansing operations at the various establishments, be affected in accordance with the subjoined regulations, which, with a few exceptions, will be found capable of general application.

That with respect to the burial ground, no interment in future take place within one hundred yards of the wall enclosing the general hospital; that no more than one layer of corpses be placed in any grave or trench; that a space of not less than twelve inches be left between each body; that the grave or trench be at least six feet below the ordinary level of the ground; that a layer of peat charcoal be placed over the bodies instead of lime; and that all interments take place during the morning or evening, and not during the heat of the day.

That with respect to the ground already occupied, a layer of peat charcoal be at once laid over it, the ground levelled, and then sown with grass seeds.

The details of the above works, as well as of those at Kulali, have been explained to Captain Gordon, R. E., your very able commanding officer of Engineers, who has expressed his willingness to carry them out.

In drawing up the preceding directions as far as they apply to the Barrack Hospital, the Commissioners have dealt with the condition of the wards and corridors as they found them. They cannot, however, abstain from expressing their opinion that the sheds which are being erected in the Barrack Square, occupy space that had better have been left vacant, as the greatest freedom for external ventilation is required.

The Commissioners are further of the opinion that not only should the number of sick within the hospital be reduced as soon as practicable, but that the corridors should be put and retained to their true use, namely: to afford means of access to the several rooms, to give protection from external variations of temperature, and to facilitate full internal ventilation.

In anticipation of the heat of summer, the Commissioners advise the removal from the building of all persons (soldiers) not necessary to the care and comfort of the sick, and that additional accommodation should be provided.

Before concluding, the Commissioners cannot but express their gratification at the zealous co-operation they have received, not only from your Lordship but from the officers of all the institutions it has been their duty to visit, Scutari.

We have, &c. (signed) John Sutherland. Hector Gavin. Robert Rawlinson.

However, things were moving very slowly. There was always red tape on where the money was to come from, what guidelines or steps to follow to address the problems, and who would be responsible. All this mayhem continued to reach the House of Commons.

'I feel hopeless and depressed; it feels like we are working in vain; until the sewage problem is resolved, diseases will continue, and we will never achieve cleanliness.'

'Listen, some of the things can be done before the sanitary commission takes any action,' Dr Pisani remarked. 'I'm here to help you.'

'Mortality rates are rising as a result of this filth, but they must act, and they must act quickly,' said Florence.

'I don't want to see you down; come on, you're exceptional at your job; let's see what we can come up with.'

'I have some money on hand that I personally gathered and received from The *Times* fund. With it, we will be able to purchase and install the boilers that will wash the clothing and linens thoroughly, as well as additional hard brushes for the floors and soap and lime for cleaning the toilets and bathtubs.'

'Tomorrow, we'll go together to check what needs to be done about the boilers. I'm here to be by your side.'

Dr Pisani helped Florence update her stocks every day, maintaining the system she developed with a stock card for each item, replenishing supplies, and preserving the records of the doctors' requests organised chronologically. In just two months, Florence was able to begin gathering inventory data. She fulfilled the medical staff's requests for slippers, nightcaps, plates, knives, forks, tin cups, and spoons in the appropriate quantity. She purchased surgical trays, clocks, towels, soap, combs, and screens. When writing to Sir Herbert and reporting everything, she went by the moniker 'The General Dealer.' The doctors appreciated Florence for organising all the supplies because they understood the effort it took to maintain such many resources for a hospital.

After what felt like an insurmountable task, cleanliness had finally become a reality. However, all this effort was not enough. The rate of death was still alarming inside the hospital.

Florence locked herself in her room so that no one could witness her distress except Dr Pisani.

'Numbers don't lie; look, I'm giving up. It's impossible; all this cleaning, and yet there is still a significant mortality rate, seems inconceivable,' argued Florence.

'The wards are rife with infections. We need to address the issue with the sewage system; when will this sanitary commission move to begin work?' substantiated Dr Pisani.

'I'm sick and tired; my soul is heavy.'

'You cannot stop now; you have gone a long way. I'm here to encourage you to keep going.'

Dr Pisani grabbed hold of the situation. The sewage system, which was seriously impairing the hospital's sanitation, had to be temporarily repaired, at least in part. So, fifty workers were hired to aid with repairs in the wards and the drainage system before more casualties occurred.

However, Sebastopol saw a steady increase in casualties. Two steamers anchored, and the sick continued to flow down. In seventeen days, it was expected that four thousand wounded soldiers would be treated.

Amid all this work, Florence's situation became increasingly challenging due to disputes between Catholic and Protestant nurses. Cases of insubordination were quickly followed by some nurses who were overtired and went inebriated, eventually becoming prostitutes for the soldiers. Florence had no choice but to act.

All those concerned were expelled by her and sent back to England. Priests, private individuals, doctors, and nurses made accusations and counteraccusations, which were exchanged between Whitehall and Scutari.

Queen Victoria reinforced Florence's position more than ever during this crisis. The Queen begged Mr. Sidney Herbert in a letter to ensure that she regularly viewed the reports and statistics produced by Florence. The Queen further stated that Florence and her nurses should convey her message to all the soldiers who are wounded or ill while serving in battle, saying that their Queen takes a warmer interest in their suffering and feels more for it than anyone else does. She thinks about her cherished warriors every day and night. Likewise, the Prince.

All the troops received this message, which was also distributed to the wards, put at the hospital's main gate, and printed in the newspaper. To Mr. Sidney Herbert, Florence wrote, 'The men were touched.' The troops said that it was a really heartfelt letter from the queen and demonstrated how much she cares about and considers her soldiers.

On Christmas Eve, Florence was given the responsibility of distributing gifts from the Queen to the soldiers. Queen Victoria was greatly influenced by Florence. The Queen responded quickly to various recommendations made by Florence, one of which was to amend the law governing sick soldiers' pay so that their pay would not be reduced once they were hospitalised. Being hurt while lying in bed was the result of heroism, so they should still receive the same compensation.

Florence almost attained the status of a goddess thanks to her composure, inventiveness, and ability to take action. The soldiers adored her, the physicians became reliant on her, and Dr Pisani was more than pleased with her. Statistics were preserved in greater detail in order to be submitted to the Cabinet in order to make particular decisions at Scutari, Balaclava, and advances in health facilities in England.

Florence and the medical staff were particularly concerned about the fact that soldiers continued to arrive at Scutari in large numbers and that fatality rates continued to rise despite obvious improvements in sanitation and nutrition. A pandemic exacerbated the situation.

The Queen received Florence's data and reports on a regular basis, and she carefully examined them. The Cabinet debated the first Sanitary Commission's report from Constantinople as well as the high mortality rates that Florence had tallied.

The final decision was made. A group of workers was to be dispatched to Scutari to work on the sewage, plumbing, and building systems to address the dangerous situations that were causing a high mortality rate among the casualties. Meanwhile, Florence's sense of failure, disappointment, and desperation grew. The more she battled and wanted to succeed to show that women could succeed, the more she felt like a failure.

Dr Pisani comforted Florence every evening as he worked to support her psychologically, physically, and administratively. A solid working relationship developed because of Dr Pisani's full faith that what Florence had accomplished so far was the most important success of all time.

When the Sanitary Commission returned to Scutari, they immediately got to work on the suggestions made during their initial inspection. Their alarming findings characterised the hygienic flaws as fatal. According to Florence, there were inadequate and overburdened sewerage systems below the building. The structure was seriously flawed. Huge sewers beneath it created cesspools full of sludge and wafted their venom into the higher rooms. The walls were covered in grime, the floors were in such bad shape that many of them could not be scrubbed, and there were countless numbers of rats everywhere. The available water was tainted and insufficient. The sewage system had to be reconstructed.

The fatality rate started to drop immediately after the impact. The situation was getting better, but Florence's critics were back in full force.

CHAPTER TWELVE

Jealousy, Hurdles and Glory

1856, the Crimea and Windsor

Florence was not only physically fatigued, like everyone else, but also mentally and emotionally upset for not having attained the results she desired. At least, that's how she saw it, even though Dr Pisani consistently refuted this and told her that she had accomplished more in the field of health than a conqueror ever could. She was already a phenomenon because she came from a wealthy and affluent background and had managed to survive under the most horrific conditions. Dr Pisani and the Queen were not the only ones to acknowledge her accomplishments; other people also acknowledged her success. The troops respected Florence and looked up to her as a mother, nurse, psychologist, and caretaker; nevertheless, her colleagues grew resentful as soon as they noticed how much better things were at the hospital. They began spreading rumours about her. They had lied about her accomplishments, and she felt duped. She consequently became fixated on her purported shortcomings. Dr Pisani, however, was constantly by her side to provide the solace she required.

More jealousy came in from the Chief of Medical Staff of the British Expeditionary Army, the senior medical officers, and medical officials who professed to be the Scutari Hospital's pillars of success. Certain individuals' treachery was injurious to Florence, as were the formal charges made by these same people to the War Office against her that she personally ill-treated and harassed them. Soon after, Florence received a formal letter asking her to adjust her behaviour. She could read between the lines as to what had transpired, but she remained silent and said that she would do everything she could to ameliorate the situation.

However, more serious betrayals followed, as reported in The *Times*. Reports were made public criticising the British Army's medical staff and officials. The devastation was immense, but Florence now wielded greater strength since she had her country with her. She was elevated to the status of a national hero because of the English people's devotion and affection for her.

A legend was born. The survivors of the British Army returned to England and told the country about what Florence had done for them and how the Barrack Hospital had been transformed. Florence was in every British national's heart and on their tongue. Every cottage, tenement, court, tavern, conference, and the House of Commons hailed her.

Florence's achievements inspired biographies and songs. Prints of her portraits were made, and visitors to her Embley home asked to see her desk and where she lived. Journalists flocked to her home in Embley to question her relatives. Her tireless efforts, hardships, illnesses while serving in the Crimea, recoveries, and unwavering dedication to her work until the end of the war gave the people reason to believe that her contributions would be recognised on an official level. A Nightingale Fund was shortly formed as donations began to stream in. The funds were to be used to establish a nursing training institution.

Queen Victoria, to mark her warm feelings of admiration, wrote,

Queen Victoria to Miss Florence Nightingale. Windsor Castle, January 1856.

Dear Miss Nightingale,

You are, I know, well aware of the high sense I entertain of the Christian devotion which you have displayed during this great and bloody war, and I need hardly repeat to you how warm my admiration is for your services, which are fully equal to those of my dear and brave soldiers, whose sufferings you have had the privilege of alleviating in so merciful a manner.

I am, however, anxious about marking my feelings

in a manner which I trust will be agreeable to you, and therefore send you with this letter a brooch, the form and emblems of which commemorate your great and blessed work, and which, I hope, you will wear as a mark of the high approbation of your Sovereign!

It will be a very great satisfaction to me, when you return at last to these shores, to make the acquaintance of one who has set so bright an example to our sex. And with every prayer for the preservation of your valuable health, believe me, always, yours sincerely,
Victoria R.

The brooch, designed by Prince Albert, carried the dedication, *'To Miss Florence Nightingale, as a mark of esteem and gratitude for her devotion towards the Queen's brave soldiers.'*

Florence wasn't thrilled; compliments, admiration, prints, diamonds, medals, and other items didn't move her. Nothing could now make up for the suffering she and the medical staff had endured. They continued working until the last patient left the Barrack Hospital on July 16, 1856. The war has ended. A formal proclamation of peace was confirmed during a peace summit in Paris.

Florence and Dr Pisani were the last two medicals to leave the Barrack Hospital. They gave their final orders to the staff workers who were still cleaning the wards. They turned to look inside the structure once more before departing, but this time it was silent and devoid of the cries of the injured. The voices of agony that wouldn't stop revering in Dr Pisani and Florence's minds accompanied them as they arrived at Constantinople's pier. There, they found their ship waiting to take them to Valletta so they could travel to Marseilles. A Queen's emissary met them prior to boarding.

Given that it was a Mediterranean summer, the journey was peaceful. Florence frequently dragged herself out on deck since it was oppressive to stay inside the ship. Normally, Dr Pisani would go with her since he was concerned about her health, which had gotten worse due to all the stress, illnesses, and horrific experiences she had been through.

The ship sailed for two weeks before reaching Valletta's Grand Harbour. Florence reached into one of her pockets and pulled out a note for Dr Pisani. 'You have my address on this piece of paper; we'll keep in touch,' she says. He knelt on his knee and kissed her hand; she was crying. Dr Pisani grabbed his suitcase and dashed down the ship's passageway, signalling a coachman to take him home.

At this point, Florence's mother and Parthe started to wish for her return. They were unsure how to greet her. Similarly, the country was fervently eager to honour her. Mayors were secretly attempting to find out where Florence would first set foot on English soil upon her return, and entire regiments wanted to send their bands to welcome her.

Florence set out for Paris after arriving at the port of Marseilles, where she spent one night before setting sail for England the next day. She travelled north by train to Calais and then over the English Channel to Dover by herself. The Convent of the Bermondsey nuns was her first destination after arriving in England. She arrived on her own, rang the bell, and was welcomed to spend the morning in prayer and meditation with the Reverend Mother. Florence appeared to be in good spirits, but her health was significantly compromised. Her body was very thin, and when by herself, she was very depressed. She didn't like her celebrity and was terrified of it, so she kept this journey a secret; it took her another twelve days to arrive.

The two housemaids were working on some stitching in their room at the front of the house when one of them looked up and saw a vision of a woman wearing black approaching them. Her sister Parthe, mother Fanny, and her father, William, were in the drawing room.

One housekeeper motioned with her hand towards the person walking outside and said, 'Look,' to the other housekeeper. 'It's her,' one of the housemaids gasped, and both fell into tears, sprinting out of the house, reaching Florence, snatching her suitcase, and shouting, 'She is back, she is back!'

CHAPTER THIRTEEN

Salvatore Luigi Pisani

1856, Valletta and Paris

Florence adhered to her word, and she was grateful to Dr Pisani for being a great motivator. The day after she arrived, Florence sat down at her desk in her room and started writing a letter to Sir William Reid, the governor of Malta, regarding Dr Pisani. While she was still at Scutari, she had already sent letters to Sir William Reid and Sir Sydney Herbert about Dr Pisani.

Florence wanted to emphasise this time that at Scutari, other medical superiors talked highly of him, and that Dr Pisani paid exceptional attention to his professional work. She went on to remark that, despite his youth, he deserved to be promoted and given a high rank.

Dr Pisani was only twenty-eight years old, but his bravery in the medical field was a trait passed down from his family of doctors. At the age of sixteen, on October 1, 1844, Dr Pisani strolled from his house on Strada Alessandro to Strada San Marco in Valletta and entered a little bottega called 'Galea's Studio' for a picture as a remembrance of his first day of university. After receiving his doctorate six years later, he went to L. Preziosi in Floriana for the graduation photo while donning his cap and gown.

Dr Pisani resided in a richly decorated house on the northern edge of the city with his parents. At that time, Valletta served as the focal point for all activities in Malta. The bells of St. John's Cathedral sounded every day, and the cannon salute often accompanied them when important individuals embarked. The Strada Reale was constantly busy. The pavements were filled with riflemen in red-jackets and green uniforms. They were all scanning the area for beautiful, enigmatic Maltese women wearing black faldettas, hoping to make eye contact with one of them to learn more about their sweetness and brush off their shyness. The little island of Malta was unable to accommodate the influx of troops that were arriving at its port of call before departing for their mission. People were offered all kinds of homes, including the Auberges of the Knights, the Forts of St. Elmo, St. Angelo, Fort Manoel, and Lazzaretto, as the hotels Imperial, Dunford's, and Baker's were all fully booked. The old, creaky steamers that anchored at Grand Harbour were constantly bringing soldiers and their families to Malta. Every ship that arrived was a cause for excitement for the Maltese. Children ran hastily with mums following them to the *Barrakka* to view the vessels docking, then walked down to the customs house landing to witness the disembarkation of wealthy people wearing feather hats and quality fedoras.

Raising your head and looking around, you could see residents of Floriana, a walled suburb city, squeezing out of their windows and balconies to be the first eyewitnesses to the newcomers. The disembarkation of passengers from ships was clearly an exciting event for the locals. People were bored, and they had nowhere to go. Even the soldiers experienced this. Malta didn't have much to offer; the opera theatre consistently presented the same two works, Trovatore and Norma, both of which were poorly performed, except for the orchestra's outstanding effort. There were just a few locations outside of Valletta: St. Paul's Bay in its natural seas, Citta Vecchia—Mdina, the Garden of St. Antonio, the Capuchin Mortuary, and once again inside the city, St. John's Church. The monotony was in the air, with troops and people standing on the steps of the clubs, sipping coffee and eating ices at Café del Commercio. People strolled up and down to the post office to see if their mail had been sorted and if they had any, or they were just there to peek at the noticeboard, which was constantly updated with information on public notices and which vessels were arriving and going.

The Strada Merkanti was at its best. Blue and silver fish, amazingly sized vegetables, piles of figs, delicious, sweet grapes, melons, peaches, apples, and oranges—an abundance of brilliant colours. The street stalls resting against the richly carved stones were accompanied by bright-eyed, smiling, picturesquely attired sellers.

In other streets, herds of goats were taken door to door to be milked. The goats had red scarves around their necks and a little bell hanging from their collars. Valletta was the island's commercial centre, with vendors trying to sell their horses or donkeys for transit and transportation in every corner of the city or sell rides on their carts with a cushion for the ladies to sit comfortably and hearing the coachman saying, 'Carrying a lady best, madam.'

During his studies, Dr Pisani would spend hours in the shady Valletta during the hot summers. He enjoyed his routine of walking to Strada Stretta for a look at Mr. Quintana's library and then to Marsamxett to rent a boat and visit his classmates in Msida.

On this island, there wasn't much going on. Dr Pisani wanted to make more progress in his education and disease-related research. His goal was to graduate and travel abroad to gain different hospital experience. His accomplishments were noteworthy, and he was successful in realising the goals he set out to pursue. He had not even had time for his graduation portrait to be developed when he left for Marseille and Paris to deliver his cholera research.

He initially travelled to Edinburgh after meeting other doctors in Paris who encouraged his studies and research and offered him opportunities to work in their labs. His thesis, titled 'Epidemics of Cholera in Malta and Gozo,' was presented to the university while he was enrolled in the MD programme with a focus on chronic diseases.

However, Dr Pisani always felt compelled to go back to his native country because he felt obligated to improve the health of the Maltese people. On the other hand, he consented to travel to the Crimea because it was important for his personal goals to broaden his own knowledge spectrum away from Maltese shores.

Dr Pisani was designated medical officer in command of the St. Julian's camp a week after his return from the Crimea, even though he was still recovering from some of the illnesses he encountered there. The Maltese were proud to have a courageous doctor who exemplified professionalism and dedication. As a result of his work alongside Florence Nightingale in the Crimea, Dr Pisani gained popularity in Maltese society, and his name began to appear consistently in newspapers.

Florence and Dr Pisani communicated frequently. In their correspondence, they discussed matters such as surgical techniques, hospital ward upgrades, disease research, and complete manuals on how hospitals should run. They had to put into effect everything they had learned from their experiences.

Two months after they returned from the Crimea, Florence addressed a letter to Dr Pisani, inviting him to visit England because they had both been summoned to a private meeting with the Queen. The royals, Queen Victoria, and Prince Albert, wanted to hear their experiences firsthand and examine their reports, research, data, and studies. Queen Victoria prioritised the army's health as well as the health of the general populace, and as a result, she intended to reveal significant hospital advancements to the entire nation.

So, in September of the same year, Dr Pisani sailed on the P&O Marseille line, the first cargo carrier ship enroute to Marseille. He had grown accustomed to living without necessities by this point and didn't give much thought to sharing a tiny cabin with three other sailors for sleeping. Dr Pisani seized the chance to offer his assistance to the crew, where he discovered some of them suffering from cholera and helped and treated them. The rest of the team wasn't in the best of health either because poor sanitation frequently led to infections and illnesses. People's lack of understanding of what constitutes a clean, sanitary environment was to blame for the lack of sanitation. So, until he reached Marseille, Dr Pisani's responsibility was to encourage and treat anyone on board while also trying to educate them about the value of cleanliness.

The ship finally berthed at the old harbour at the break of dawn on the twenty-fifth day at sea. Dr Pisani collected his belongings and medical case and hopped onto the shore, exhausted and hungry. He hurried swiftly in the direction of the horse-drawn carriages that were waiting to provide rides to anyone who inquired, and he stopped in front of the one that appeared to be the most comfortable and was pulled by six horses.

The coachman opened the carriage door. Dr Pisani said as he got in, '*A' Paris.*'

It was a one-week journey, but he knew where to eat, sleep, bathe, and rest.

He had previously visited Paris. Prior to his departure for the Crimea in 1854, he had already visited a few medical facilities in 1853 and joined the German Medical Society in Paris. Dr Pisani made some acquaintances at the inn and even bartered his medical skills while he was there, so his expenses were kept to a minimum. He stopped in Arles to send a letter to Florence at her friend's Paris address, to notify her that he had arrived. At Clarkey's home in Paris, Florence was waiting for him. She fled Embley in stealth to Paris because she disliked being noticed. Florence told her family about her trip, but pleaded with them to tell everyone that she was still recovering in her room. She did, in fact, require more rest and a longer period of recuperation, but the meeting with the Queen had to go on. Thus, she left her father, William, attempting to keep the journalists beyond the main mansion gate, while her mother and sister were occupied sorting through her mound of arriving letters.

Dr Pisani made additional brief stops in Avignon and Vallon-Pont-D'Arc, where he met an alumnus of Edinburgh University. He then travelled to Beaune, Lyon, Fontainebleau, and Paris before being greeted by

Florence at Mary Clarke's home. Dr Pisani and Florence both considered Paris to be their second home, where they had many high-profile acquaintances. It was a treat to dwell in Clarkey's home in the heart of Paris. At her 120 Rue du Bac salon, Mary Clarke was still the salonnière, organising conversations and welcoming authors, leaders in thought, presidents, orientalists, and economists. She was always a stunning, stylish woman who attracted men, regardless of her age. Dr Pisani was equally impressed by her beauty. He only met Mary Clarke briefly during his stay at her Parisian home. She had too many commitments and was too busy. She would arrive home in the middle of the night or stop by for a bath and to change into something appropriate for the ball, concert, or whatever political event she was attending. Mary Clarke knew Florence was very busy preparing for the Queen's meeting, so she didn't bother her much during her visit, except for a dinner she scheduled with Florence and Dr Pisani the night before they departed for England. They talked about their present affairs here. Mary Clarke was telling Florence about the politicians she was working with in the House of Commons, giving her the names of major figures in the health industry and some background information.

'Louis Blanc has fled to your homeland.'

'Ah, really, looking for success or an escape from facing failure?'

'He is a quiet, compiling historian works and shuts himself away.'

'I don't expect him to be like that for long.'

'No, no, surely not, he told me he will return to France and will again be in politics.'

Mary Clarke turned to Dr Pisani to advise him on what she had heard so far as Malta was concerned.

'The course of the last few years has brought about a rapid amelioration on the island, whereby the mode of life is almost entirely comparable to that in England and France. The island's meteorology is attractive; no place can boast of a greater equality of temperature. Throughout the winter, an entire day without sunshine or an entire day of rain is equally rare, although it does occasionally occur. This makes Malta popular as a place of residence for invalids.'

'Yes, in fact, I've read Dr Sankey's report quoting that the Maltese winter is soft and balmy, and several invalids, with dry coughs and bronchial irritation, have expressed themselves as always feeling better when they spend the winter in Malta than when they spend it in other places.'

'Another advantage which Malta possesses over almost every other place is the great facility which the invalid has of getting away, should he find, or fancy he finds, the climate uncongenial to his constitution. The almost daily arrival and departure of English, French, and Italian steamers will enable him to try other countries, make excursive trips, and again return as frequently as he wants.'

'Truly, I have known people whose health has been considerably improved by residing for a while in Malta and making short voyages to the neighbouring countries.'

'Malta is a medicine in itself,' intervened Florence.

They continued to converse about their visit with the Queen, the financial and economic conditions of both nations, and, most importantly, how they planned to move forward in their personal and social lives. Conversations over dinner and the exquisite wine that was provided by the staff lasted until late, after which it was time to retire to bed.

A horse-drawn carriage approached Clarkey's house at the crack of dawn. Dr Pisani and Florence crept out of the home while the city was still asleep and climbed into the carriage. As Florence correctly adjusted her attire in the coach, she grinned at Dr Pisani. The coachman hoisted the goods onto the top of the carriage, then gave the horses the reins and sent them galloping. They had a long journey ahead. However, when compared to what they had experienced at Scutari, simply sitting down and conversing and stopping at towns and villages for meals, rest, and sleep was a luxury.

CHAPTER FOURTEEN

The Meeting with The Queen

1856, Balmoral

When they arrived in the port of Dover, it was crowded with ships, some of which needed repairs. The area smelled strongly of sulphur from the smelting activities. A coachman and one of the Queen's messengers were waiting for them. On their faces, their weariness from the journey, the restless nights, and what they had experienced at Scutari were evident. Their memories of the hell they had witnessed in the Crimea were still vivid. Both felt haunted and pursued by things that happened right in front of them. After all this hardship, it was now their responsibility to inform the Queen of these self-evident truths. The testimony of Florence and Dr Pisani would confirm that the hospital systems were to blame for the high death rate.

They had a long journey from Dover to Birk Hall. To continue the journey, the coachman had to stop at inns to relax and change horses. Florence and Dr Pisani, on the other hand, delved into their reports, statistics, and correspondence during each stop to ensure that everything was prepared to be presented to the Queen.

Along the way, they would discuss whether to include more notes in their reports; the plan was clear: they would request the establishment of a Royal Commission to investigate the sanitary condition, administration, and organisation of barracks and military hospitals, as well as the organisation, education, and administration of the Army Medical Division.

Colonel Tulloch was to join Dr Pisani and Florence at Sir John McNeill's home in Edinburgh where they were to stay first. For some time, Florence and Dr Pisani worked in the Crimea with Sir John McNeill, a surgeon, and Colonel Alexander Tulloch, a great War Office administrator who served as the regiment's captain. They both reported on the setup and administration of the commissariat, the method of keeping accounts, and the reasons behind the delays in unloading and distributing clothing and other stores items sent to Balaklava. Therefore, it was crucial that they all get together before the meeting with the Queen to go through everything that will be presented.

A couple of days later, Florence and Dr Pisani left Edinburgh for Birk Hall, the Highland home of Florence's longtime friend Sir James Clark. As a highly respected physician, Sir James Clark was chosen to serve as the Queen and Prince Albert's Physician-in-Ordinary in 1840, as soon as the Queen ascended to the throne. He was appointed the monarch's closest medical counsellor. Florence and Dr Pisani once more discussed the presentation to the Queen with Sir James Clark.

They spent two days going over each note and report, the statistics, and the ideas being proposed. Florence did receive some advice from Sir James regarding the presentation, and he also reminded them of proper protocol when they would meet the Queen.

Sir James Clark escorted Florence and Dr Pisani to Balmoral, in the quiet, tranquil valley of the River Dee in the foothills of the Grampian Mountains, for an afternoon conversation with the Queen and the Prince. In the breathtakingly luxurious drawing room, which was adorned with paintings from bygone centuries, everyone was welcomed by Queen Victoria and Prince Albert, a charming couple who were already parents to eight children and two months pregnant.

'Your Majesty,' said Florence, bowing her head and curtsying.

Dr Pisani followed them, and they all sat down at the dark-oak dining room table. There, they spread out documents containing information about the hospitals' structures, notes, statistics, and financial reports.

'So, what am I to be aware of? Please explain thoroughly what these papers tell,' uttered the Queen to Florence and to Dr Pisani.

With complete openness, Florence started outlining the statistics and reports on the operations, infrastructure, and systems of the hospital.

This informal meeting lasted more than three hours

and was a great success. Florence won the monarch's admiration. She had laid out all the flaws in the military medical systems as well as the necessary improvements.

Queen Victoria and Prince Albert were so impressed by Florence and Dr Pisani that they were summoned to Balmoral on two other separate occasions while staying at Sir James Clark's mansion. They engaged in a wide range of conversation topics, including war, religion, metaphysics, and the pregnancy of the Queen. A friendly, trusting relationship grew. Dr Pisani and Sir James Clark were given permission to question Her Majesty on the pregnancy's progress. Dr Pisani felt extremely honoured by this.

In addition, the Queen paid secret visits to Sir James Clark's home. In the early afternoon, Florence spotted the Queen approaching in her little pony carriage. The monarch invited Florence on walks and afternoon tea conversations. Her bravery won the Queen's heart.

This was only the beginning, though. They realised that the Queen, in her position of authority, could only listen and accept, but she couldn't act. They required the Ministers of the Crown to begin taking action on these ideas and proceed forward.

As it turned out, Lord Panmure was expected at Balmoral. He acquired the nickname of 'the Bison' due to his large head, which was covered with dense hair and which he tended to rock from side to side. During the final stages of the Crimean War, Lord Panmure served as the Secretary of State for War. He received harsh criticism for essentially doing nothing. His motto was 'don't initiate any action, so no consequences arise.' Procrastination was his idol. This stolid Scottish nobleman was not someone who would easily be pushed. He was more than willing to accept the need for reform 'in principle,' but he lacked any internal driving factors and needed to be physically prodded into action. It was therefore an uphill struggle to overcome Panmure's procrastination, but the Queen persisted, and she wrote to let him know that they would be meeting in Balmoral. Colonel Tulloch, Sir James Clark, and Sir Sidney Herbert all had doubts about Lord Panmure's decision to adopt Florence's suggestions. The meeting was scheduled for October.

Nonetheless, Dr Pisani couldn't stay in the Highlands until October since Sir William Reid had notified him that his services were urgently required in Malta. During his last informal dinner with the Queen, Dr Pisani presented her with a gold filigree cross of the Knights of St. John as a token of his deep gratitude. It was a touching and unforgettable emotion to be a part of this outstanding initiative for all these health improvements that, hopefully, will be implemented not only in British military and non-military hospitals, but also around the world. In fact, Dr Pisani promised the Queen that once the Royal Commission gets underway, he will make it a priority to ensure that its changes are implemented in the Maltese health sector as well.

Dr Pisani yearned to go back to the Maltese Islands

so he could carry out his work mission there. Florence agreed to write to him and notify him of the outcome with Lord Panmure. It was an emotional departure; the proposals they had made so far in the health sector were incredible accomplishments, but the meeting with Lord Panmure would be a watershed moment for what was to come.

The conversation with Lord Panmure took place at Balmoral on the fifth of October. The Queen, Prince Albert, Sir James Clark, and Florence were all present and seated around the table in the drawing room. 'Lord Panmure.'

'Your Majesty,' Lord Panmure said, bowing his massive hair head.

'I must clarify that the status of our hospitals is impracticable at the moment. Drunken staff members, prostitution, filth, sewage, filthy conditions, a lack of medical supplies, and other deficiencies should all be a thing of the past.'

'Ma'am, I understand all of this.'

'I anticipate that you will begin providing me with comprehensive briefings on the hygienic status and general condition of our hospitals in your capacity as Secretary of State of War. The findings of your inspection and opinions, as well as a list of everything that must be done, whether in the form of arrangement, a decrease in the number of patients in the wards, cleaning, disinfecting, or actual construction, in order to secure the major goals of safety and health, must be laid before Lord William Paulet, Admiral Grey, or Lord Raglan, as the case may be, or such individuals as may be appointed by them to that special duty, as soon as possible.'

'I understand that my responsibility is to succinctly state whatever you believe will contribute to the preservation of health and life and to firmly recommend that it be adopted by the authorities.'

'There is no more time to be wasted; you may postpone providing me with reports for now and instead provide me with a list of the immediate tasks that need to be completed. You will receive Florence's statistics and reports so that you may better comprehend the urgent problems that require your attention.'

'Yes, Ma'am, I will start working right away to address the urgent priorities, remove the inconsistencies, and adhere to the standards. Due to Florence's extraordinary success, it was decided that the Royal Commission would be established by experts in the health field who had been given the go-ahead to implement the guidelines and regulations that Florence had established.'

Lord Panmure paid Florence a discreet visit in the late evening of that same day, while she was packing her bag to depart Birk Hall by morning. She was given the opportunity to address a report to Prime Minister Lord Palmerston. The first general military hospital was also being built, and Lord Panmure pledged to send her the designs. He also encouraged her to make observations and said he would be happy to make any additional improvements she requested.

All in all, this was a victory for Florence. The incredibly laborious job finally appeared to be paying off. She boarded a hansom cab the following morning to travel south on her own. Her mind was racing with ideas, and her sleepiness had shown itself to the point that it was exhausting for her to clasp her fingers around a pen to write, despite the fact that putting pen to paper in a driven carriage was not an easy chore. Florence did, however, manage to jot down the names of those who would make up the Royal Commission. She had compiled a balanced list of commissioners, civilians, and military personnel. Leading sanitary authorities, surgeons, medical professionals, service members with experience in army welfare work, a pioneer in the field of statistics, and herself were all on the list.

Setting up this Royal Commission still required a lot of work. It was difficult to expect these people to devote their time to a commission that required many additional hours of work on top of their regular jobs. All of them needed to be persuaded to give their consent and share their information, as well as gain knowledge about the reforms that some of them were still unaware of and their significance.

During her travels, Florence continued working to set up the commission. She wasted no time. She understood she had taken a significant stride forward in the health sector in words, but there was still much work to be done to turn those words into action. Florence continued to push forward with her plans.

When she finally arrived at the Embley mansion, she was greeted by her parents and sister. Florence, exhausted and falling into her father's arms, exclaimed that she was pleased with the reforms she was instilling in the minds of the leaders and authorities.

CHAPTER FIFTEEN

The Reform

1857, London, House of Commons

After two years of hurdles and failures, the Royal Warrant to establish and launch the Royal Commission was finally granted. The news delighted Dr Pisani. Florence had succeeded in what she believed in; now it was Dr Pisani's turn to ensure the success of this Royal Warrant in Malta.

It turned out that 1857 was a year of accomplishments for Dr Pisani. He was assigned to the chairs of anatomy and histology, midwifery, and gynaecology at the University of Malta after leaving the British army with a stellar reputation. He had recently turned thirty.

In the same year, the Royal Commission, in accordance with the Royal Warrant, created laws governing the army's sanitary condition, the organisation of military hospitals, and the treatment of the sick and wounded. Florence appointed Dr Pisani to supervise and support the Army Medical Officers stationed in Malta in understanding the significance of and adhering to these restrictions.

Lord Panmure addressed the opening report of the Commission to the Queen,

'VICTORIA, by the grace of God of the United Kingdom of Great Britain and Ireland, Queen, Defender of the Faith,

To Our right trusty and well-beloved Councillor, the Right Honourable Sidney Herbert; and to Our trusty and well-beloved Augustus Stafford, Stafford, Esquire; Sir Henry Knight Storks, Knight Commander of the Most Honourable Order of the Bath, a Colonel in Our Army, and Secretary for Military Correspondence in Our War Department; Andrew Smith, M.D., Director-General of Our Army Medical Department; Thomas Alexander, Companion of the Most Honourable Order of the Bath; Sir Thomas Phillips, Knight; James Ranald Martin, Esquire, F.R.S.; Sir James Clark, Baronet, M.D.; and John Sutherland, M.D.; greetings.

Whereas it hath been humbly represented to us that, considering the great importance of maintaining and improving the health of all ranks of Our Army, at home and abroad, and of providing for their medical care and treatment in cases of disease, wounds, and other casualties whatsoever, in the most approved manner, it is expedient that certain inquiries should be made into the constitution of the medical department of Our Army, the mode of appointment of its officers, and the system which regulates their rank, pay, promotion, and retirement; likewise, it is further expedient to examine into the condition and administration of the hospitals of Our Army, with a view to their increased efficiency.

Now know ye, that we, having taken into our consideration the premises, do hereby order and direct you the said Sidney Herbert, Augustus Stafford, Sir Henry Knight Storks, Andrew Smith, Thomas Alexander, Sir Thomas Phillips, Sir James Clark, James Ranald Martin, and John Sutherland, to inquire into the organization, government, and direction of the medical department of Our Army.

And firstly, to inquire into the mode by which candidates for first commissions are selected, and the system adopted for their promotion and routine of service; also, the mode adopted regarding their pay and retiring allowances.

And further, we do order and direct you to inquire into the means now adopted for acquiring, keeping up, and adding to the professional knowledge of the officers of Our medical department, and to consider whether it will be expedient to encourage them to combine civil practice where compatible with military duty.

And further, we do order and direct you to inquire into the operation of the regulations now in force, with a view to the prevention of disease in Our Army, both at home and abroad, as regards barrack accommodation, encampments, clothing, rations, and other matters relating thereto, having regard to the various climates to which Our troops are exposed, and the duties and responsibility of the medical authorities on these matters. And further, we do order and direct you to inquire into the state and condition of military hospitals, both general and regimental.

Also, into the system adopted in the same, for the treatment of Our soldiers, and the powers possessed or exercised by the medical superintendents or other functionaries in such hospitals, for providing diet, medicines, and every requisite for the medical and surgical treatment of the patients under their charge, together with the character of the diet, medical comforts, furniture, and other hospital supplies.

Also, we do further direct you to inquire generally as to the expenditure of such hospitals, and the financial control now exercised in and over the same, and the relative authority of the various departments whose functions are exercised within the hospitals.

And further, we do order and direct you to inquire into the rules and regulations, or the practice, in force for invaliding and discharging the soldiers of Our Army, when brought forward for discharge, as unfit for future service. And further, we do order and direct you to inquire into the system of management and treatment of and the provision made for patients in civil hospitals, whether in immediate connection with Our Army or otherwise, and to consider whether such management or treatment, or any portion thereof, can be introduced with advantage in the medical department of Our Army. And we further order and direct you to inquire into the expediency of making provision in Our military hospitals for the officers of Our Army suffering from disease or accident incurred in Our service, and to consider whether it will be advisable to provide in Our military hospitals for the treatment and cure of lunatic officers or soldiers, or to establish a separate military hospital or hospitals for that purpose, or in any other manner to provide for the treatment of such cases.

And we do further command and require you to report what changes you may consider expedient to make in the organization, management, and expenditure of the medical department of Our Army, with a view to the utmost efficiency of this branch of Our military service, and what measures you may recommend being adopted, with a view to the preservation of the health of Our troops at home and abroad; and also that you do report your opinion upon such returns or records as should be kept by the medical officers of Our Army, with a view to the preparation of a well digested and accurate body of military medical statistics.

And it is our further will and pleasure that you, or any five or more of you, do obtain information touching the matters aforesaid by the examination of all persons most competent, by reason of their knowledge, habits, or experience to afford it, and also by calling for all documents, papers, or records which may appear to you, or any five or more of you, calculated to assist your researches and to promote the formation of a sound judgment on the subject, and that you, or any five or more of you, do report to us, under your hands and seals, your several proceedings, by virtue of this Our Commission, together with your opinions touching the several matters hereby referred for your consideration..

Given at our Court at St James's, this fifth day of May, in the year of Our Lord one thousand eight hundred and fifty-seven, and in the twentieth year of Our reign.

By Her Majesty's Command. (Signed)
PANMURE.

The Royal Commission then released a comprehensive report with data, hospital floor designs, and pay scales. Florence was transforming the private reports she had written over the years into a significant book that the Commission could read, act on, and publish. *Notes on Matters affecting the Health, Efficiency and Hospital Administration of the British Army* was the title of her debut publication. With all the real facts, Florence was the Royal Commission's leader, armed with all of the genuine facts.

Florence and Dr Pisani were both under a lot of pressure. Dr Pisani, who, in addition to his regular duties, was working hard to provide Sir William Reid with the information from the Royal Commission regarding the new rules governing the medical division of the army. Later, the same procedures would be replicated and required to be followed by non-military medical hospitals as well, since Dr Pisani felt compelled to develop public hospitals that were now lacking in everything but the most fundamental necessities. And it was here that Dr Pisani took the first steps towards civil hospitals and the health of the Maltese people.

In the military and civil hospitals, medical staff training was to become standard practice. With the aid of Florence's advice and guidance as well as his own expertise, he put together the curriculum for the new School of Practical Midwifery. In an attempt to establish a school, he used a room at the General Hospital and first invited staff members who were already employed in hospitals to attend some of his lessons. However, after a year of instructing nurses and other medical personnel, there was a lack of participants, and classes were stopped.

Furthermore, Dr Pisani sent a report to Dr G. P. Portelli, Comptroller of Hospitals and Charitable Institutions, along the same lines that Florence had written for the military hospitals. According to Dr Pisani, the Maltese people also deserved a hospital that was organised rationally. The purpose of Dr Pisani's report was to promote a restructuring of Malta's public health system and health laws. As Florence did for the military, the report indicated the need for a new overall management strategy for the jobs in the organisational structure and their responsibilities.

Following that, Dr Pisani addressed the subject of the hospital buildings. According to Florence's *Hospital Notes*, he advocated a structural reform in hospitals for the Maltese and discussed with senior health officials that the current Central Hospital at Floriana was inadequate. This hospital was originally a building built by Grand Master De Vilhena in 1734, known as the Conservatorio, originally set up to house pauper girls and teach them various crafts.

It was made abundantly clear that it was not the right hospital structure and detailed all its drawbacks as well as suggestions for reform or new hospital construction. This hospital was already overcrowded for the entire Maltese population; in addition, sewage was constantly pouring from the structure, flowing below it, and being drawn into its thick walls, spreading disease. Dr Pisani faced a significant hurdle from the Maltese health authorities, and he understood that only time would allow his spoken and written reports to be accepted. He received encouragement from his father, Luigi Pisani, who was the Central Hospital's superintendent at the time. His father agreed with him that what he was insisting on was right and precise; he had encountered circumstances in hospitals just as horrifying as those his son had witnessed.

Florence and Dr Pisani experienced difficulties, disagreements, objections, and arguments every day. Putting all these measures in place was a big undertaking that was not universally welcomed.

At this point, Florence had already started advocating the legalisation of civilian hospitals in England. Letters from Dr Pisani poured in, describing the complete anarchy he witnessed in hospitals as well as the ignorance, foolishness, intoxication, and harsh customs that infected them all. Every hospital staff reported the same tumultuous circumstances and conditions. Staff have even prepared Florence reports to give her a complete picture of the realities of these infirmaries to assist her in pushing for the necessary legislation and eventually presenting it to the prime minister.

She started working on a reform plan from her room in Embley as she was still healing and battling tiredness and the illnesses she had contracted in the Crimea. Such plans were to be forwarded to Dr Pisani as well, giving him a constant reform strategy for Malta's civilian hospitals. This would greatly aid him in his discussions with the comptrollers.

Luigi Pisani, the father of Dr Pisani, passed away in 1865. While working at the Central Hospital, he had been exposed to typhoid. This affirmed that hospitals were not a place for the sick to recover but rather a place where they would deteriorate and ultimately pass away. The passing of Dr Pisani's father served as evidence that working in hospitals may be fatal.

CHAPTER SIXTEEN

The Wedding

1870, Valletta

Dr Pisani kept a careful eye on one of his students. He'd seen him several times while walking with his cousin, Giovanna Micallef, in Valletta.

Young males generally viewed courting women as a professional move rather than a romantic one. It was usually done in stages. Initially, couples would meet up only to chat. Later, they would start going out together. Finally, after both parties had established their shared attraction, couples would keep in touch for longer periods of time. Giovanna, his cousin, was apparently already engaged in a second stage of romance, according to Dr Pisani.

'Oh, good morning, Lorenzo!' Dr Pisani exclaimed cheerfully as he welcomed Lorenzo into his classroom and turned to close the door.

'Good morning, sir. I have some medical questions for you, please,' Lorenzo said.

'Of course, tell me, but first, I have something to

tell you. I noticed you strolling with Giovanna; you know she's my cousin.'

'Yes, I know; it's the first thing she told me when I started going out with her,' Lorenzo said while blushing.

'You're a hard-working student, Lorenzo. Your high grades are above average, and since you've chosen to focus on eye diseases, you have a bright future in ophthalmology. Remain focused on your academics.'

'Oh, without a certain doubt, falling in love with Giovanna does not imply that I shall be distracted from my educational pursuits.'

'I know you are a mature, responsible intellectual, so I didn't intend it at all.'

'I wish to extend my studies, possibly even abroad. That's what I'm striving for—meeting other medical professionals with whom I can exchange experiences. Then I'll return and marry Giovanna.'

'Oh, what wonderful news! It's lovely when two people meet and realise they can spend their entire lives together. I will assist you with finances when you travel abroad, as well as with contacts, as I know several doctors in both London and Paris. with the prerequisite that...'

'That?'

'You will marry Giovanna when you return.'

They smiled with dazzling excitement at these remarks, and Dr Pisani added, 'Now tell me, what queries do you have?'

Dr Pisani was overjoyed to learn about his cousin's

wedding. In his life, he now desired to have experiences that would alleviate his pain from the agonies of hell witnessed at Scutari; they were haunting his head. Florence was worse because she was now declining, even physically. They kept up their constant correspondence and offered consolation to one another for their experiences. Florence always said that Hampshire's tranquil countryside was beneficial to her health.

This prompted Dr Pisani to begin seeking a home outside of Valletta's crowded city walls.

Dr Pisani told a friend about his desire to purchase land in the countryside, and the friend recommended him to Dr. Degaetano, a notary and solicitor.

'I have a client who owns a sizable piece of rural land in the south of Malta.'

'I'd be interested to see it.'

On the same day, the doctors boarded a Maltese horse cab, *Karozzin,* from Valletta to the village of Zejtun, and after passing through this settlement, they arrived at a large field area designated for sale on Dr Degaetano's drawing plans. They got out of the cab and began walking alongside the fields' *rubble walls*, holding the plans open. Then Dr Degaetano said, 'Here, somewhere here, it seems all this area; this route then takes you downwards to Marsascirocco's second settlement, the fishing village.'

'It's lovely here; I like breathing the air of peace,' said Dr Pisani as he walked down the edge of the land specified on the plan. 'The price?' he asked.

'That I don't know; we need to talk to my customer about it. We should head back to Valletta so we can visit his residence. What I do know is that he wants to sell it because he needs the money to purchase a retail establishment in Valletta.'

They went thereafter, and after speaking with the owner face-to-face, Dr Pisani settled on a price. The following day, the owner and Dr Pisani were seated in Dr Degaetano's office, writing the contract of sale.

Dr Pisani walked home, satisfied with the purchase of this land, and drew a rough drawing of the mansion he had always imagined, where he could rest, read, study, write, entertain visitors, and have all the amenities he deserved, including stables, horses, and a *remise* building.

Meanwhile, Giovanna and Lorenzo were hunting for a home as well. They didn't want to stay at their parents' houses since they desired that their house also welcome patients and function as a clinic for Lorenzo's work. Dr Pisani was so eager to assist this couple that he promised to bequeath his home in Valletta to them and then relocate to his new home in Marsascirocco once it was completed. His parents were both with the Lord, and this property, which he received as the sole son, would be an ideal gift for this couple.

The relationship between Giovanna and Lorenzo was seamless. As was customary for a gentleman, Lorenzo pushed for a marriage date as soon as possible before he left once more for his research in Paris. Without any hesitation, Giovanna set the date for November 22, 1870. St. Barbara's Church in Valletta was chosen as the venue for the wedding, and the bride's parents' home would host the reception because it was a sizable aristocratic home and could accommodate a good number of guests.

Things were getting ready. As a seamstress, Giovanna had a keen sense of style. Giovanna designed the bridesmaids' gowns. The grenadine fabric was used for all the bridesmaids' and bride's white outfits. Although it was pricey, Giovanna could afford it. She compiled her trousseau with the help of her parents, filling it with outfits appropriate for the social status of both her and her future husband. It was essential to have high-quality, long-lasting bed linens, towels, curtains, and other household décor. She didn't need much, as the property was already stuffed to the gills with elegant furnishings, but carpets and home décor were added to decorate the space.

As was customary, Giovanna and her mother made house calls to their wedding guests and friends. The bride's house was also getting ready for the wedding party. In the drawing room, a table was put up to showcase the couple's gifts from guests, as well as thank-you notes for the gifts and some mementos of the occasion.

Guests usually used to spend some time at this table evaluating the gifts and congratulating the bride. During the final month leading up to the wedding, fresh flowers were often ordered. Flowers were to be placed at the house entry and in the drawing room, particularly on tables, side tables, and other furniture; in other words, flowers were to be abundant everywhere the guest set foot.

The day of Lorenzo and Giovanna's wedding came, and horse-drawn carriages began to appear in front of Giovanna's home. The words *hierga, hierga*, 'here she comes,' echoed throughout the neighbourhood as everyone waited at their front doors, on the pavement, and along the street, some on their balconies and windows, with flowers in their hands to throw as an augur. Then, there was a wave of applause and a hooray, followed by flowers falling from the sky and children running to gather the flowers from the ground before someone stepped on them while competing to see who gathered the most.

The bride, her parents, and one of the bridesmaids rode in the bride's carriage. Following were the other carriages carrying the bridegroom's mother and other family members.

Before the bride arrived, the groom, Lorenzo, entered the vestry with his 'best man,' who had already arrived at the church. The priest performing the ceremony made a few last-minute arrangements on the altar, and Dr Pisani, who was serving as a witness for Giovanna in this marriage, was already seated on the first bench and revising the passage of scripture he would read during the mass celebration.

The Church of St. Barbara in Valletta is a Baroque-style church with an oval dome, typical of the period but a very rare feature in local churches. It was built in 1573 to serve the spiritual needs of the knights of Provence and was known as the church of the bombardiers. It was restored in 1601 and completely rebuilt in 1739. The exterior of the new Church of St. Barbara was designed by the Italian architect, Romano Carapecchia, while the interior was designed by the Maltese architect, Giuseppe Bonici, as Carapecchia died before the church was completed. Its plan is based on the oval shape, which is contained in the narrow rectangular site, with a less centralised interior. The oval shape of the church is extended eastward to an enlarged area containing the high altar. The painting on the altar depicts the 'Martyrdom of St Barbara' in oil on canvas on commission from Fra Filipp Wilhelm von Nesselrode-Reichenstein, the Grand Prior of Allemagne in the Sovereign Military Order of St John. In 1739, the project was completed.

The choir was resonating the hymns that would be sung during the wedding, and the chapel was decked out for the occasion with white daisies and roses along the pews and on the altar. People began congregating both inside and outside the church. The ground was shaken by the sounds of horses and the rumble of wooden wheels. The carriage arrived at St. Barbara's church, and Giovanna walked up the aisle, her arm around her father's arm, the bridesmaids following her, accompanied by Schubert's Ave Maria sung by the church choir and the maestro on the church organ. Lorenzo stood at the altar, grinning and concentrating on Giovanna as she came up to him and took a seat to his left. She also had her bridesmaid within reach behind her, to whom she had given her left-hand glove and bouquet. As was customary, Lorenzo took off the glove from his right hand to get ready for the vows. It was a lovely wedding service with prayers, gospel readings, and a sermon interlaced with balanced humour by the clergyman that made everyone grin, with the acme being 'the vows' uttered by the young couple.

As the ceremony came to a close, the bridesmaids stepped up to distribute wedding favours to the attendees before they left the church. When Lorenzo and Giovanna walked up the aisle to exit the church, they were met by the congregation on the church steps and Strada Repubblica. They could now converse with them to express their gratitude for their attendance. The attendees reciprocated by wishing the newlyweds well. The high social position of the guests that Lorenzo and Giovanna invited—notaries, lawyers, doctors, university professors, and foreign medical researchers—reflected the social class that the new couple would be residing in.

Lorenzo and Giovanna were honoured with a ride in the romantic carriage around the city, overlooking the majestic and spectacular grand harbour, to give ample time for the invitees to gather at Giovanna's parents' house for the wedding fête. The house was packed with family and friends recounting events, hugging, wiping away emotional emotions, and sipping branded liquors and spirits. There was an abundance of food and drinks. Three frenetic hours had been spent by the servants in preparation. They now served an entrée of a well-seasoned fish soup (*aljotta*) or a vegetable soup (*minestra*), followed by a second course of various flavoured meats ranging from mutton to stewed rabbit, lamb to braised beef, spiced tongue to spring chicken, accompanied by the house's best white and red wine.

The cake, which was standing tall, dressed entirely in white, and placed in the centre of the table, ready to be sliced and served, was the *pièce de résistance*.

The bridesmaids' task was still not done. She escorted the bride out of the reception while the cake was being served, getting her ready to shed her wedding gown and put on her honeymoon dress.

After a few minutes, Lorenzo noticed Giovanna's absence, which meant she had retired, so he bid his companions a tearful farewell. Giovanna, returning in her newly updated look and clothes, said goodbye to the bridesmaids and lady guests while sobbing and taking one last look at the house she was about to leave.

The servants ventured to swarm her with their humble yet genuine compliments. Finally, she sobbed on her mother's bosom, and her father led her out of the house to hand her to Lorenzo, her husband, who assisted her in climbing into the carriage waiting for them to take them to 33, Alessandro Street, their residence, which, for the time being, would be shared with Dr Pisani until his Marsascirocco house was ready to greet him.

CHAPTER SEVENTEEN

The Arrival of the Sepoys

1878, Valletta Grand Harbour

The sepoys, fighting with the ferocity of wild creatures, their eyes scowling with wrath and fanaticism, were crumbling in the face of their opponents' cool fearlessness and grim determination. Half-distracted women were seen mingling in the fight, hoping to save a beloved husband or relative, and terrified children were seen running wildly here and there, but unmolested, because they were everywhere respected and saved. The British soldier fought to the death against the ravisher and the murderer but respected the women and children even in the heat of vengeance.

The brutal clashes between the British troops and the mutineers in Delhi in May 1857 were a horrifying display of the bloodshed and miseries of war. In British newspapers, vile accounts of massacres and atrocities were widely disseminated. Her Majesty's forces required assistance.

Britain sent more troops to India and eventually succeeded in putting down the revolution, resorting to harsh tactics to restore order. Delhi, India's capital, was in ruins. The sepoys surrendered in their thousands. Calm and tranquilly became the norm by 1858. The British administration implemented reforms, including religious tolerance and the recruitment of indigenous people into the public service. While the reforms aimed to stop similar uprisings through conciliation, the British military in India was bolstered because the British thought that their interests were in danger and the government needed to act.

Hospital reforms then followed. Since the 1600s, Indian doctors and surgeons have collaborated with British medical professionals. Priority was given to the establishment of civic, military, and medical services. The country was massive, and the need for health care was overwhelming. A Health Commissioner and a Statistical Officer were appointed in India in 1868 with the permission of the Royal Commission in accordance with Florence's reforms, which were implemented to ensure consistency and order in the medical field wherever British troops were stationed.

Florence's spirits were raised when Mr. Herbert paid a visit to Embley to notify her about the selected committee in India.

'If I'm permitted to travel to India and provide immediate aid, then...'

Sidney Herbert interjected, 'Take that thought out of your mind, you won't physically travel to India. You are too weak to travel that far. With your gallantry, you have already helped enough troops.'

'He's right, my dear,' said her father.

Florence was aware that India was still far behind, but her health was failing, and she wouldn't be able to handle the pressure of travelling so far.

Florence Nightingale's thoughts, however, were constantly on India. According to the reports she had received from Sidney Herbert's office, the sick troops' high fatality rate was shocking. She wrote letters to the Council of India, a member of the Royal Commission, from her home in Embley, asking for statistical data, but the data collected was false and inaccurate, lacking relevant facts and records, documents, and files. The information Nightingale desired was to be gathered from third and fourth parties, if not a fifth party, as the India Council of the Royal Commission never visited India.

So she made the decision to take action from her Embley office desk. She started working before the Commission was established. She wrote a circular packed with inquiries to be distributed to each military outpost in India. As the responses arrived in the India office, they were forwarded to her for analysis. The result formed a statistical survey on which she wrote a long report entitled, with that modesty that always dictated her choice of titles, *Observations on the evidence contained in the stational reports submitted to her by the Royal Commission on the Sanitary State of the Army in India by Florence Nightingale*. This report was published alongside the Commission's, but Florence had copies bound separately, adorned with illustrations to give the reader an immediate sense of what was going on in India.

These drawings depicted the tribal practices of carrying water and sewage over long distances by hand in pails, skins, or carts before emptying them. She also provided pictures of hospital designs and new sewage system sketches to many people, including royalty.

A copy of this report was also sent to her friend, Dr Pisani, for his consideration and to better understand and communicate with the British governor in Malta about the situation in India, which was putting more strain on the military hospitals in Malta as British troops returned to Malta injured and sick in their thousands.

In the meantime, Malta had become a hive of expatriate activity. HMS *Serapis* was the iron-hulled vessel commissioned to and from India; its planned passage normally would be from England to India, passage planning took seventy days, depending on the seas and weather fronts. This time, HMS *Serapis*, the troopship, was destined to arrive at the Grand Harbour. On October 15, 1873, HMS *Serapis* commenced her voyage from India to Malta. On her journey, she collided with a French schooner in the Indian Ocean, and after rescuing the French crew, HMS *Serapis* headed to the Grand Harbour. The vessel collided again, with the British steamship *Paladine* due to the fierce wind and waves that drifted through the Grand Harbour. The

Paladine was practically destroyed, and the HMS *Serapis* needed some repairs, so she had to stay at the Maltese harbour. The landing of the sick British troops from India was done hastily to prevent the spread of diseases. They were taken straight to the military hospital and put in an isolation area to be medically examined.

The few Indian troops that happened to be under the same military regime were also transferred. Other British troops in a healthy state would go into the military camps and wait for the order of whether they would soon be moving somewhere else or sent on the voyage to Britain.

Her Majesty made the hasty decision to extend HMS *Serapis*' mission to cover the transfer of both British and Indian troops. There was a Commons debate when orders were conveyed to India calling for the initial deployment of 10,000, 20,000, or 25,000 Indian troops to Malta.

The House of Commons wanted to know whether that was the case, and when Malta was quoted, the House of Commons was reminded that they did not know whether these troops were to be sent. The Home Secretary was not able to tell them where these troops were to go. The Chancellor of the Exchequer said it was merely a movement of troops from one part of the Empire to the other; but where was it to? Was it to Aden, or Suez, or were they going to occupy Egypt? The House of Commons was entitled to know whether there was a change of policy, but the policy was to endeavour to bring about a peaceful settlement. But who believed that? The right hon. gentlemen, in the ensuing debates, might appeal to European opinion as generally supporting the policy of Her Majesty's Government. But why did the French, the German, and the Italian papers support Her Majesty's Government? Not at all because its policy was a policy of peace, but that it was a policy of menace and of war; because it was an attempt on the part of Her Majesty's Government to bring Russia's nose to the grindstone, or to force her into a long and enfeebling war, which would weaken her for generations. They were entitled to know what was proposed to be done with these Indian troops, and what were the Constitutional grounds upon which this step was to be defended. It might be true, as the Chancellor of the Exchequer had said, that the government were within their technical right in this act; but he would ask whether it was always right to carry technicalities to extremes. In a free nation such as Britain, looking to the jealousy with which any extreme action on the part of the Monarchy was regarded, the Government might take it upon itself to push the limits of constitutionalism too far; and to advise the crown to push its technical rights to the very verge of un-constitutionalism was a very serious step, and might do that which would, by-and-by, shake the stability of the throne itself.

Following Her Majesty's decision to send the Indian troops, the operation began in 1878, when some eight thousand sepoys boarded the HMS *Serapis* and sailed for Malta, along with almost one thousand horses, ponies, and bullocks. Russian forces had invaded Europe through the Balkans and compelled Turkey to sign the Treaty of San Stefano, but they were stopped by Great Britain, which organised her forces and sent sepoys from India to Malta.

However, if Great Britain can keep Russia advancing in the direction of the Mediterranean, Russia could be able to fundamentally undermine British rule in India. The British would suffer since India was their sole available source of new labour for the armed forces. The Maltese were concerned about the number of sepoys that had just disembarked and how they would adapt to Malta. At the customs wharf, an echo of Maltese whispering, *'Indjani, Indjani, intlejna'*, 'Indians, Indians, overcrowded us' could be heard.

It was impossible to observe Indian and British or French troops stationed together. The Maltese couldn't figure out yet how these Sepoys, with their different customs and religions would settle. The Maltese found the Indian garb weird because of the colourful turbans they wore on their heads, even if the rest of their uniform was similar to the British one with blue pants and red jackets. The Maltese were unhappy that so many other cultures were permitted to coexist with their own, but they were unable to do anything about it other than gossip and spread rumours.

However, because the Indian troops were part of the British military, they had already become accustomed to British customs and routines, except for those regarding the adoption of religion and self-discipline. Wherever the sepoys went, they still assembled and made their religious pilgrimages, and they were pleased with their daily food of grain, pulses, and water, remaining quiet, submissive, and polite to their superiors.

In stark contrast to all of this was the British soldier, who was overcome by inebriation, discontent, and disobedience. Even if the Maltese culture inherited a sinful behavioural legacy from the British soldiers' vices, the most disciplined character—the Indian—was undoubtedly not warmly received.

The cousin of Queen Victoria, The Duke of Cambridge, Prince George, sailed to Malta to visit the troops. HRH Field Marshal the Duke of Cambridge assessed the army during the Floriana Parade in Malta on June 17, 1878. They were all Indian infantry, with the exception of the two Royal Artillery batteries. The Duke was very impressed with their demeanour, training, and camp setup. Their next stop was Cyprus, which Turkey had given to Britain as part of a covert agreement in return for support against Russia.

It had been two years since India had been declared a British colony, affirming Queen Victoria to be 'Empress of India'. Yet, a lot of questions were debated during the Commons sittings.

Why the decision of Her Majesty's Government to dispatch a force of Indian native troops to Malta was not communicated to Parliament before the rising of the House for the recess, the public announcement that that step would be taken having been made the day after Parliament separated for the holidays.

The Chancellor of the Exchequer was prompted by the sitting to answer that he could only say that the decision of Her Majesty's Government to order a certain number of Indian troops to Malta was one arrived at some time ago; but that it was not thought necessary, nor was it according to practice, that such a decision should be communicated to Parliament. It would, however, be their duty, as early as was convenient—and hopefully to be done very soon—that they lay before Parliament an estimate of the cost of that expeditionary movement; and that would be the most convenient time for raising any discussion it may be thought desirable to raise upon the subject. There was no doubt whatsoever that this was a very important step; but it was, at the same time, a step which, after all, when you come to regard what it was, was neither more nor less than a direction given by Her Majesty for the moving of a portion of Her Forces from one part of the Empire to the other. And though it was a movement which would undoubtedly come under the notice of Parliament, and over which Parliament held the control, which it held over all movements of British Forces—that of the right of withholding or challenging the supplies asked for the purpose—yet, so far as the order given to Her Majesty's troops was concerned, it was an order strictly within the proper constitutional prerogative of the crown, and one which Her Majesty had as much right to give as to order any portion of British troops now in England to proceed to Gibraltar, or Malta, or anywhere else.

The House of Commons insisted on the debate of these troops and their expense. As the third reading of the Customs and Inland Revenue Bill came on that evening, they wished to know how the right honourable gentlemen proposed to provide out of the ways and means of the present year for the expense consequent upon withdrawing these troops from India. Was the necessary expense to be met by a fresh loan or by additional taxation? These were all questions to be fulfilled and the transferring of troops had to be made more precautious so as not to create a negative result of an enormous increase in the financial burdens of India. Such things should be debated well between Her Majesty's Parliament and the House of Commons before the attainment of decisiveness and authoritativeness.

CHAPTER EIGHTEEN

Residing at Marsacirocco

1878, Marsacirocco

As Dr. Lorenzo Manche conducted ophthalmology research in Paris, Dr Pisani was there to assist him. Due to the contaminated water supply on the Maltese islands, which had caused numerous cases of trachoma, ophthalmology had been a top priority for public health issues on the islands. Even though ophthalmology was not his area of expertise, Dr Pisani nevertheless wanted to assist Dr. Lorenzo in his academic and research activities because it would provide him with a career boost. Dr Pisani, on the other hand, was determined about returning to Malta to fulfil his commitments, which by this time had grown to include giving lectures at the University of Malta as a Professor of Anatomy and Histology, Professor of Midwifery and Gynaecology, and Professor of Surgery.

His next objective was to start writing books on health and midwifery. Dr Pisani longed for the completion of Villa Sans Souci, where he would undoubtedly find peace, quiet, and his own time to relax, write, and work.

He anticipated having more control over his personal time and routine. He'd missed this since sharing his house with Lorenzo and Giovanna. Because his life was demanding, Dr Pisani understood the importance of living a balanced existence that included both work and downtime.

The remaining mahogany Victorian furniture requisitioned by Dr Pisani was moved inside the house the day before the Sette Giugno. The housekeeper led the carpenters through each room. With the assistance of Dr Pisani's cousin Giovanna, the tailor was still finishing up the heavy window fabrics for the curtains. The beautiful wool floor carpets and druggets were rolled flat on each floor by two other ladies, who also helped Giovanna in organise and harmonise the furniture placements in each room. Giovanna was entrusted by Dr Pisani to do the task successfully. He didn't have time to worry about any of this, so he just picked the latest materials and styles and left the rest to his cousin. Giovanna approached this endeavour with all her passion out of respect and gratitude for everything that Dr Pisani had given to her and her husband, Lorenzo.

The following day, Dr Pisani entered Villa Sans Souci. He now felt as though he had everything he required in this home to lead a comfortable and serene life. Indeed, the tranquil and quiet atmosphere was the first thing that struck him. There were no longer any sounds of city life surrounding him. He slumped backward onto one of his fauteuil armchairs, closing his eyes, taking a deep breath, and giving thanks to God for everything he had been through and achieved. At this precise moment, he felt within his own body a liberation from all the stress accumulated over the years. Turning his head to the side, he noticed a decanter of Scotch Whisky, stood up, filled a glass halfway, raised the glass, and exclaimed in French, *'Je lève mon verre à la liberté,'* a cry for liberty.

The few seaside residences that made up the tiny fishing village of Marsascirocco were once only built as a secure storage area for small boats or fishing nets. However, some of the fishermen later made the decision to occupy these structures. The anglers had been granted permission by the British government to use these as their homes, saving them from having to travel from Zejtun, where they had their own house, to Marsascirocco. This decision by the authorities prompted more people, including other anglers, to relocate to this village, build homes, and live there. Marsascirocco was established as a village in the latter half of the 1870s.

People from neighbouring villages would travel to Marsascirocco harbour, either on foot or by horse and cart, to barter or buy fish, especially on Sundays and feast days. The freshly caught fish was being sold straight away from the recently moored *luzzus*. The famine was at its peak. The impoverished people, with no money or anything good to barter, would leap into the sea to stay close to the boats, waiting for a misfortune to the hardworking fishermen, that some fish would slide back into the sea from the overcrowded boxes, and then they would capture it back with a swift stretch of the arm to feed their family.

Life at Marsascirocco was dawdling. With their young children, women in their modest homes passed the early morning hours while leisurely grinding African coffee beans on the porch step or strolling through the winding lanes between the fields while toting on their heads the clothes they had just washed in a nearby natural spring at Casal Zejtun. Men were repairing and prepping nets as others sanded their boats in preparation for a fresh coat of paint. You could smell the aroma of baking bread and cooking food from miles away. Life was straightforward, modest, and guiltless.

The strenuous schedule followed by Dr Pisani was significantly dissimilar from the Marsasciroccons' way of living. In any case, Villa Sans Souci was a very secluded and far-off location. At the mansion, Dr Pisani had two people he could rely on. One was his coachman, who oversaw setting up the horses and carriage each morning and generally maintaining the stables, and the other was the housemaid, whom Giovanna hired to handle all of the general housekeeping. After breakfast, Dr Pisani would leave early for Valletta, where he would give a lecture at the university or attend to his necessary responsibilities at the Central Hospital. Dr

Pisani's days at the university and Central Hospital, the two most challenging institutions in the city region, were filled with encounters with a variety of people, from students to professors, as well as dealing with patients and other medical professionals; as a result, his routine of work required that, after hours of hard work, he would return to his magnificent, serene home, which had by this point become an oasis of recuperation for himself. The largest garden behind Villa Sans Souci, which was near a vast expanse of agricultural fields, was where the most tranquil moments occurred. The garden featured fences, walkways, arches, and a gazebo made of limestone. A trellis that adorned the walkway leading to the gazebo and a profusion of ornamental plants combined to create a lovely ambiance. Before reaching the gazebo that was located at the far end of the garden, a clever succession of lemon, orange, and mandarin trees were planted on the other side of the passage. Here, to the singing of various birds making their homes on some of the trees, Dr Pisani spent most of his time reading and creating his own writings as he savoured the glorious all-seasonal days that only Malta could give. The housemaid would frequently notice that Dr Pisani had fallen asleep and would need to be woken up for dinner. He had made it a practice to conclude each day after dinner by sitting on the garden bench and gazing at a lace of leaves until the final light of the sunset hung between the trees.

Since his first years at the university, Dr Pisani has

been collecting antique coins. But now that his collection included historical medals of the Order of St. John of Jerusalem in addition to coins from the Punic Age, Roman era, Order of St. John, French, and British eras from George III to Queen Victoria, it was a collection that had greatly expanded in both its quantity and, most importantly, wealth, and deserved a whole room on its own, with specialised showcases designed by the Professor himself, so each collector's item could be displayed in style. Dr Pisani would spend hours examining his collection, keeping track of all the coins, and looking for new treasures to add to his personal collection. In fact, the Professor's wealthy collection prompted him to build the iron gates at the stairwell to separate the first floor of the home from the basement portion of the house. When guests were welcomed to Villa Sans Souci, these gates were kept locked, and this did cause invitees to draw back and retreat when they noticed such seclusion upon entering the hallway. In order to divert guests' attention away from the gates and instead direct it to the beauty of other artefacts, Dr Pisani had the brilliant idea to paint some alfresco scenes on the walls of the hallway leading up to the stairwell.

CHAPTER NINETEEN

The Stealthy Journey

1878, London to Valletta

Since she returned from the Crimean War with 'Crimean Fever,' Florence was apparently experiencing health issues. According to reports, she never fully healed, was unable to walk, and was bedridden. Such accounts were somewhat exaggerated because she was experiencing symptoms of extreme stress, physical exhaustion, and dreadful visions of the events she had witnessed in the Crimea, but she managed to continue.

She did make a covert trip from Embley to London and back. She travelled by train with the assistance of the platform crew and under her aunt's supervision. She was developing legendary status. She journeyed in order to publish her writings so that the House of Commons would have a solid basis on which to discuss the issues raised by the ongoing changes in healthcare infrastructure. She also wanted to meet influential people who she knew would act appropriately to alleviate the situation.

Dr Pisani worked closely with the British Governor for the Civil Hospital for many years. He was a member of the Barrack and Hospital Improvement Commission, which was led by Sir George Cornwall Lewis and Lord Sidney Herbert, both of whom collaborated with Florence in the Crimea and in London. When Captain Douglas Galton and Dr. John Sutherland, two members of the Royal Commission, visited the Maltese military hospitals and met with Dr Pisani, the representative of the commission for Malta, it appeared that several improvements in the drainage system, water supplies, and sewage disposal were crucial. Florence's comments on hospital renovations made note of these modifications as well as the absence of windows and ventilation shafts.

Captain Galton, Dr. Sutherland, and Dr Pisani's report from 1869 made it abundantly evident that there was a need for suitable hospital accommodations for military patients. As a result, they formally suggested in a letter and report to the Royal Commission that a new hospital be built. Dr Pisani also had in the back of his mind Civil Hospitals, which were more subpar than Military Hospitals, but Military Hospitals were more urgent than Civil Hospitals. The general public had to wait. Malta was under British colonial administration, and the British were the first to be served. Dr Pisani was quite irritated by this because he placed a high importance on the health of the Maltese people. Such sentiments were expressed to Florence, but she was always emphatic in telling Dr Pisani that even in England, the military hospitals were the priority, followed by the civic ones.

The Collector of Land Revenue told the Chief Secretary to the Government on November 16th, 1870, that three plots of land had been purchased at Cottonera, contracts had been approved, and the sites were now available to the military authorities for the construction of a new hospital. Captain Douglas Galton of the Royal Engineers created and built the hospital. He was the army's leading specialist on barrack construction, ventilation, heating, water supply, and drainage. He was a superb young engineer. He was a member of the Barrack Commission, had a significant War Office position, and served as a referee for the review of proposals for the drainage of all of London. He was also by this time related to Florence's family because, in 1851, he married the lovely Marianne Nicholson, Florence's cousin.

The infrastructure of hospitals was a topic of frequent meetings and correspondence between Florence and Douglas Galton.

'I have roughly but accurately sketched how to prevent foul air from being blown into the hospital wards. The water closets and bathtubs are completely walled off from the wards by a ventilation system that makes sure any unclean air is forced outside of the ward. They are located at the corners of the wards, across from the entrance. The huge end window is crucial since it makes nighttime ventilation simple.'

'I'll be able to include anything you've sketched. Your previous experience in medical facilities serves as my model. I want this hospital structure to be successful in terms of design and construction, but also to make sense in terms of health, with a focus on ventilation in particular to prevent sickness,' said Douglas.

'An open window is never a bad thing. It is the remedy. One window for every two beds, opposing windows in each major ward, and a divide between the hospital proper and the administration are among the ideas contained in this plan. Additionally, there should be no more than two floors of wards.'

By the end of 1873, Cottonera's building construction project had been completed successfully, and it was regarded as one of the best hospitals in the central Mediterranean.

The situation was just the opposite in the civic hospitals, where chaos, disorder, and confusion were growing. The number of sufferers had grown. The difficulty of isolating the infected cases grew as a result of the decision to accept all contagious cases of measles, scarlet fever, diphtheria, and whooping cough at the Central Hospital rather than continuing to use the subpar Santa Spirito Hospital. Some patients had to be housed in the hallways due to the male surgical division's overcrowding. The Commission of Maltese Physicians and Dr Pisani made recommendations for a larger structure to take the place of the Central Hospital.

'We understand your suggestions, but there is no funding available for this project,' responded the Comptroller of Charitable Institutions.

A decision like that made Dr Pisani defiant. 'The mortality rate would go down if we could just improve the hospital and provide more care for the patients, as our people are suffering and dying.'

Unfortunately, many lives were not rescued in time since the Maltese health system could not keep up with the demand.

When the Cottonera Hospital was fully operational, Dr Pisani went to Preziosi, a photographer at 19 Piazza Bretanica, Floriana, and asked him to come take some pictures of the hospital at Cottonera so he could send them to Florence. And so, it was. 'I look forward to seeing you here in Malta to show you around this hospital, which, after all, is your original masterpiece,' Dr Pisani wrote in a letter to Florence after the photos were developed. He wanted her to know how well the hospital was doing. He enclosed the photos with the letter.

Florence and Dr Pisani continued to write each other letters. Finding a letter from Florence in his box at the Valletta Post Office was something he longed for. He typically picked up such letters in the early morning before going to the college or the Central Hospital. At the Auberge de Castille, where his carriage would stop, he would express his gratitude to the driver, and proceed on foot to Banca Giuratale, the primary post office along

Strada Mercantile.

Five years had gone by when Dr Pisani picked up a letter from the Central Post Office, dashed outside in Strada Mercantile while unfolding the paper, and quickly read it. His face lit up, crow's feet appeared around both of his eyes, and a broad grin took hold of his features. He received a letter from Florence informing him that she was enroute to Malta.

On board *Le Caire*, a French vessel bound for Malta, Florence encountered Monsieur Polignac, the grandson of Prince Polignac, whom she knew had served in the French army in the Crimea. The *Le Caire's* deck was covered in cushions of every shape and colour, so Florence and Monsieur Polignac chose to lounge on the cushions there rather than enter the crowded area under the deck. The risk of infections, particularly cholera, was great, so it was safer to stay on the outdoor deck, even though the searing sun was painful and the summer night breeze was divine. When they arrived in Malta, where the August heat was oppressive, they didn't know how they would have survived the suffocating heat if it hadn't been for the iced lemonade and iced water that Florence and Monsieur Polignac found waiting for them at the nearest Grand Harbour Inn. Florence was helped by Monsieur Polignac and an officer to travel to The Imperial Hotel at No. 91 Strada Santa Lucia, where she intended to stay until Dr Pisani was made aware of her presence in Malta. Florence requested a pen and paper from the hotel employee behind the desk at the reception.

'I'm at The Imperial Hotel, Florence,' she wrote, and she gave the note to a young staff member of the hotel for a shilling to post it in Dr Pisani's mailbox at the Post Office.

The following morning, Dr Pisani discovered the message and hurried to The Imperial. When he arrived, he asked for Florence and was told to go to the hotel's garden, where he discovered her reading the newspaper at the breakfast table.

CHAPTER TWENTY

Viva La Vida

1878, Valletta

It was impossible to miss Florence's serene expression. She was at ease in Malta. She was extremely familiar with the nation. The Maltese were kind people, with everyone willing to help. The streets of Valletta were often busy. Beginning in the wee hours of the morning, a herd of goats could be heard ambling around the streets while ringing the silver bells that hung around their necks in preparation for milking. There was a medley of passersby, from introvert women under their black faldettas to sandaled Capuchin friars on their way to St. John's Cathedral and coachmen on *karozzini*, smoking, laughing, and singing as they went along.

The sound of the carts' wheels bearing their cargo for sale, from reels of fabric to carpets, chicken eggs to rabbits or hens in cages, and then the scent of kerosene when the cart with the kerosene tank approached. Occasionally, a cannon salute from the Fort echoed within the city walls.

City walls created small lanes, some ascending by steps, with buildings high up to third-floor levels, with balconies extending over the tight streets to give residents a sea view. All day long, beggars were everywhere. Poor individuals in rags, some mourning their poverty while others have bright, grin-filled faces, amusing themselves with the difficult aspects of their lives, and are content to have just a few coppers jingling in their pockets. Boys begging for money while half naked and in poor condition, calling out 'Miserabile' to wealthy onlookers as they pass by, or dashing and turning head over heels to attract more attention while continuing their appeal for charity. Poor fellas! Florence captured all of this from her room's balcony before heading down to the *salle-à-manger*.

This hotel served breakfast that was both French and English in style. Florence set the newspaper down and stretched to embrace Dr Pisani.

'Oh, how well I feel seeing you in person!' Dr Pisani exclaimed as he hugged Florence tightly.

'Likewise! Do sit down; coffee or tea?'

'The coffee scent is enticing me to go for its aroma,' Dr Pisani said, smiling and turning to take a warm croissant from the centre plate while thanking the waitress. 'So, how are you feeling? Are there any new pains since when you last wrote to me?'

'Oh, my pain! It has been and always will be. My recovery is not on my agenda, and I will always have wear and tear, but I am thankful that I gave my own strength and energy to everything we have achieved.'

'Your actions have earned you a lot of honour.'

'I'm now following India, but Mr. Herbert forbade me from going there.'

'He made the proper decision. You have provided more than enough to save all of these troops.'

'And even more need to be spared. In India, we have selected commissioners who are hard at work supplying the hospitals with the notes and instructions we have provided. There is always opportunity for advancement and more effective techniques and procedures to enhance the service. The way I'm being served in this hotel, perhaps everyone will be served this manner when it's most required. I'm not advocating for luxury, but rather for high standards of dignity.'

Dr Pisani looked at his watch while nodding in agreement with what Florence had just said. He had to leave so that he could deliver a morning lecture at the college. She declined his invitation to go with him as she was still physically exhausted from the sea voyage. Dr Pisani told her to get ready to check out of the hotel at noon. Florence would be greeted and accommodated at Villa Sans Souci during her stay in Malta, and his coachman would be waiting for them outside the hotel.

Dr Pisani set off for Strada San Paolo around half past noon, where he found his coachman seeking refuge from the August sun, which at that time of day transmitted its heat like steam under the skin. When Dr Pisani approached him, he was sipping some cold lemonade he just bought from an adjacent inn.

'To Strada Santa Lucia, where Florence is waiting for us,' ordered Dr Pisani.

'At your service, sir,' responded his coachman, draining the last drop of lemonade and setting the drinking tin near his feet. He grasped the reins, and off they went.

Florence was waiting for them at the hotel's entrance. Dr Pisani and a hotel employee helped Florence get into the carriage; she gave the coachman her suitcase to keep next to him in the coach box, and they left.

It was a pleasant trip from Valletta and Floriana to Marsascirocco, where they left the city and its sounds behind and entered the labyrinth of winding lanes among the fields. They passed by tiny, populated villages like Paola, Tarxien, and Zejtun before arriving at Villa Sans Souci and its tranquil atmosphere. While the coachman was preparing to stop the carriage in front of the stables, Florence turned to look at the villa with considerable curiosity and satisfaction. She was taken aback by and immediately drawn to this stunning property.

Dr Pisani unlocked the carriage door and descended the carriage steps before turning to face Florence, who was still seated on the bench, and offering her his hand to assist her in standing up and taking a slow descent of the narrow wooden steps. She thanked Dr Pisani for guiding her to the front patio and up to the door, which was ajar and afterwards opened further by the housekeeper who had arrived to greet them.

The housekeeper bowed her head. 'Welcome; this is a wonderful honour for us.'

'I'm grateful, my dear.'

'To the drawing room,' Dr Pisani instructed the housekeeper, 'please assist her as she's a bit tired. I'll help you as well.'

Florence was led into the drawing room, where they assisted her in settling down on the velvet burgundy couch in front of the sculpted limestone fireplace. The windows were all open, allowing warmer outdoor air to infiltrate and create a calming ambience. At the same time, the room's high ceilings produced a cosy, cool atmosphere. Dr Pisani sat down on the armchair and faced Florence, who was at this time observing the Victorian décor in the room and recalling how at Embley they also had a side table like this one that she used as a desk. She praised Dr Pisani for his home and wished him success and wealth.

The housekeeper had quietly walked to the kitchen to prepare a refreshing drink for Florence and Dr Pisani, as they requested. She made two huge glasses of cool ice water and squeezed fresh lemons from the garden. Providing guests with ice was a luxury. Only the elite possessed it, and since the time of the knights, such extravagances have been prevalent in Malta.

Indeed, it was the knights who carried ice to this island from the ice tunnels on Mount Etna's slopes. *The*

Tartana della Neve (the boat that carried the ice) would transport it to Malta's Grand Harbour after being crushed, bundled in sacks, and dragged to the coast on mules. The ice would be transported from the shore to the 'Snow Depot' in East Street, close to Victoria Gate. Ice was expensive and was purchased in bags, which Dr Pisani kept in the underground wine cellar beneath the kitchen, flanked by the coolest walls of the wells built beneath the garden, from whence the water for the entire house was extracted on a daily basis.

The drinks were placed on a silver salver in front of Florence, together with a small silver rack containing tasty little sandwiches, a lovely porcelain bowl containing a mouthwatering traditional *bigilla*, a fiery broad bean dip, and Maltese water crackers, known as *galletti*. This was a respite from the oppressive heat outdoors and the exhaustion Florence was experiencing as a result of her body's constant aches brought on by the long hours she had spent working in the Crimea and the lack of sleep. A protracted discussion regarding the recently constructed military hospitals, the Royal Commission's tactics, the suffering in the civil hospitals, which were still in poor shape, and various other topics followed. Florence's eyelids grew heavy, and somnolence began to rule in that serene and tranquil setting.

Dr Pisani encouraged Florence to go to her room with the housemaid to rest on her bed while he dealt with a patient with health concerns who had to visit him at his house. Florence consented and raised herself gently with the aid of a walking stick that Dr Pisani had given her as a gift for the honoree. Then Florence carefully followed the housekeeper and clung to the stair railing as she ascended to the first floor. Through a corridor at the far back of the house, she arrived in a room that was beautifully decorated with fresh flowers, a central Victorian double bed made of rosewood and dark mahogany, a canopy made of luxurious ivory damask, and the bed covered with marcella, a white fabric in a honeycombed style with white fringes at the edges.

Florence needed assistance with her suitcase from the housekeeper, who also helped her reach the bathroom door. She also wanted to have a bath before resting in bed, so the housekeeper prepared the long nightgown that was set aside in the wardrobe next to the bed for her. The housekeeper encouraged Florence to use the bell that was on her nightstand if she needed anything. After receiving a heartfelt thank you from Florence for her patience, the housekeeper left the room to carry on with her duties.

Florence's forty winks in her bed seemed like she'd slept for a long time. The peace that dominated her mind and body was genuinely divine. More so than at her home in Embley, she felt comfortable and at home. The view of the golden and deep brown fields surrounded by skillfully made rubble walls, the bright blue skies, and the salty air blowing from across the sea of Marsascirocco was a perfect blend of calm and tranquilly. Malta served as a haven for her.

The silence was broken by the housekeeper's knocking on the door and Florence's response to come in. The legendary lady was later invited to a reception downstairs in the drawing room.

CHAPTER TWENTY-ONE

The Way Forward

1878, Marsascirocco

Florence stayed in her room, consolidating some of her writings and making a list of things to do and people to contact when she returned to England. It was clear that preparations were well under way downstairs from the pungent scent of burning oil lamps and beeswax candles. She could also hear the maids' voices as they went about their duties. The aroma of freshly cooked pastries created a comfortable, welcoming atmosphere throughout the mansion.

She continued to write while the light from the window faded in the evening, but when it became a little darker, she rolled up the papers she was working on and set them aside before heading to the wardrobe to get dressed for the reception down below. Horse-drawn carriages could be seen approaching her room through the window, and the rumbling carriage wheels disrupted the stillness that surrounded this magnificent mansion.

Glasses clinking, laughter, enthusiastic discussion, and whispering voices could already be heard. Florence dressed, combed her hair, took a quick glance in the full-length mirror, and she was ready. She didn't care about her appearance because she was too attractive and appealing when she was younger, but those days were passed, and her focus was on the pressing needs in the health sector. She was not content because there was still much work to be done.

She unlocked the door, picked up her walking stick from her desk, and went down the hallway to the landing, where she had a bird's-eye view of the people who had assembled. When Florence started to descend the stairs, a collective 'here she comes' hissed like a gust of wind and put an end to all the chit-chat. Arriving at the mid-landing of the stairs, Dr Pisani raised his glass, and everyone else did the same, shouting 'Vive Madam Nightingale.' Florence smiled and gave everyone a quick nod in appreciation as she made her way to the entrance to the drawing room.

Dr Pisani was smiling and nodding to the guests as he walked next to Florence, holding a whisky tumbler in one hand and holding Florence's arm in the other to help her find the way to the couch, which was, for the occasion, placed on a dais close to where the quartet was playing. A young girl approached her and presented her with a bouquet of flowers, after which Florence greeted the guests and lavished praise on Malta's healthcare system.

She kept her speech brief since she wanted to spend more time mingling and getting to know each visitor. Florence always seized the chance to meet new individuals and pay attention to their perspectives in order to gain knowledge from them, and this particular situation was no exception. Dr Pisani introduced her to Lorenzo Manche, his cousin's husband and now an ophthalmologist. He spoke to Florence with a lot of assurance, relating how his involvement with other students and professors in Paris, England, and Italy after attending the university in Malta had broadened not only his experiences and wisdom but also the contacts of people, whom he mentioned in the conversation with Florence, and sparked an emotional dialogue. They alluded to persons they both knew and met in their lives, and they related their experiences with them, as well as how they helped each other in their studies and in obtaining prestigious facts, proofs, and figures. Recollections of anecdotes and reminiscences of people who influenced the lives of Florence, Dr Manche, and Dr Pisani generated a lengthy discussion.

In addition, Dr. G. Monreal, who at the time was the Comptroller of Charitable Institutions reporting to the Committee of Government of Charitable Institutions, was introduced to Florence. The Committee of Government of Charitable Institutions was, in turn, directly responsible to the Chief Secretary.

The Governor oversaw all of these roles; nevertheless, the process of revamping regulations for

Charitable Institutions was taking too long, and decisions were being made too slowly, resulting in no significant improvements in civil hospitals. Florence did request a report from Dr. G. Monreal outlining the challenges caused by the dilatory judgements and a lack of funds for the civil system. Her purpose was to compare such conditions and circumstances to those in other countries, learn from them, and, if possible, provide recommendations for improvement.

'It is critical that information be supplied prior to any actions or conclusions, as these provide me with a picture of what needs to be done.'

'Yes, Florence, I do comprehend. I have reports and records of all the civil hospitals in my possession that I can give to you,' said Dr Monreal.

'Now that the army's hospital system has been organised, I do acknowledge that the civil hospitals face an even more pressing issue. Urgency is growing as a result of the population's dramatic growth. Please provide me access to any records you maintain, and I'll help you make decisions.'

'Financial terms are the problem; they always have been. The knights appear to have had little trouble keeping their hospitals running, but the civil hospitals were always seen to suffer.'

'Finance, finance, finance,' they say. 'The issue exists worldwide. The importance of investing heavily in a nation's health must be understood by the government. What kind of nation does nothing for healthcare while investing in gold? Who is the gold that makes up a nation? The people must therefore be in good physical and mental health. Sick people, sick nation.'

With as many invitees as she could speak to, Florence continued to establish connections. She also discussed with military surgeon Major William Henry Mackintosh how encouraging military hospital statistics were, even though military hospitals like Valletta and the Forrest Hospital still needed improvements to become better hospitals in the face of the emergency issues that arose on a regular basis.

The Cottonera Hospital, which Florence planned to visit while she was in the country, was admirable with all of its setups and arrangements. Some things still required work, but overall, the military hospitals were producing fairly good results.

Florence was able to converse endlessly with all social strata of people about anything, from food and dieting to gardening to fashion, with the surgeon major, professors, and medical personnel about hospitals, contacts, and their profession. Speaking with people and eliciting their expertise was like building an almanack of awareness, comprehension, information, and knowledge. It was the way she consistently displayed a keen mind.

The quartet was playing Baroque and Mozartian rhythms. The servants serving among the guests carried tumblers on silver trays filled with whisky, gin, and vodka, cooled water, and traditional pastries. The Allegro Baroque, Polka, and The Galop were played while the young and old guests danced together.

The doors to the drawing room were both open, and a nice night breeze was gently coming inside via the wide windows and the hallway, where a fresh breeze was blowing from the garden. Some guests preferred to sip wine while seated on the benches beneath the dark blanket sky with glittering twinkles above them, while others sought romantic moments in the garden's gazebo.

That evening, Florence strolled towards the main door, which was open, and discovered Dr Pisani dealing with another professor about an old coin. Even though his collection was expanding, he never gave up looking for additional collectible coins, which were becoming increasingly hard to find. She joined the deal and surprised Dr Pisani with her desire to have that coin. Dr Pisani had done so much for Florence during their professional relationship, and she wanted to thank him by making him happy. After learning that the purveyor was more interested in bartering than money, Florence crawled her hand into her left pocket and pulled out a golden filigreed brooch with an image of herself on it. She presented it to both professors and inquired about their interest in exchanging it for the coin. The professor held it in his hands and inquired as to its opening and whether it was entirely made of gold. He held the brooch with its back to him, and Florence opened a little hook with a single click. There was a tiny bit of Florence's hair inside. He appeared to be interested in the brooch. Dr Pisani was handed the coin, and the other professor thanked them both before hurrying to his carriage.

Dr Pisani and Florence exchanged a smile before returning inside to say good-bye to the guests, the majority of whom had already left. Florence and Dr Pisani gave the last goodbyes to the remaining guests while congratulating and saying goodbye to the quartet, who were packing up their instruments in the trunk. He directed a servant to pay them before they left. Keeping his hand in his pocket and holding that valuable collectible coin, Dr Pisani gestured to Florence that they could now go upstairs and leave everything in the capable hands of the servants.

Florence eagerly accepted Dr Pisani's invitation to view his coin and medal collection. It was intriguing to hear about the history of some of the coins mentioned by Dr Pisani as well as how he acquired them. Dr Pisani put the newest acquisition in a box and assured Florence that he would clean it tomorrow before placing it on display with the others.

Even though it was getting later in the night, neither Dr Pisani nor Florence appeared to be tired. Anyway, neither of them needed much sleep because their active minds were constantly plotting new courses of action. Dr Pisani flung open the door to his bedroom, took off his jacket—it was warmer on that floor—threw it on the bed, and paced towards the side table to fill two glasses of water. Florence strode across the room, straight to the terrace.

Dr Pisani and Florence were sipping their water when a refreshing breeze from the sea of Marsascirocco persuaded them to relax in the mahogany leather-upholstered armchairs on that terrace and talk about the two important upcoming discoveries in the field of world health. The first step would be to establish nursing education courses as well as to assist women in these roles, and why not female doctors as well? The second key step would be to improve the operations of civil hospitals and possibly place a greater emphasis on the suggestion of new hospital construction projects.

They would have remained conversing on that terrace into the night if it hadn't been for the housekeeper, who pointed out that it was well past midnight and assisted Florence in making her way to her room, which was ready for sleep.

CHAPTER TWENTY-TWO

Malta – The Island of Hospitality

1878, Malta

Florence Nightingale was in Malta for the third time in her life. She was smitten. The small island's tranquilly and simplicity allowed her to pass the time in a sumptuous calm that was harmonic and pleasant.

However, the active foreign visitors who simply happened to get there due to their service in the British army or navy, or as a family accompanying them, tended to feel bored. The city was indeed bustling; as was already said, Strada Reale served as the focal point for religious events, commerce, and customary celebrations. Theatres, clubs, hostels, libraries, and post offices were all overcrowded with soldiers and their families. Outside the city, one could see Malta all at once; there were few areas where people thronged, and most foreigners professed themselves depressed.

Florence, on the other hand, had a great deal of purpose once she was here. The carriage departed Villa Sans Souci for Valletta in the morning shortly after breakfast, together with Dr Pisani. The Sacra

Infermeria, which has been in operation since the Knights of St. John, was where she wanted to begin her journey. In fact, Florence was intimately familiar with the hospital; in her book *Notes on Hospitals*, first published in 1859 and now in its third edition, she recommended that a new General Military Hospital should permanently replace the Valletta Hospital. However, the hospital that was supposed to be constructed at the bottom of Melita Street, facing Marsamxett Harbour (the book also included the architect's site plans and designs), was never built. The construction and relocation of the new hospital at Cottonera took fourteen years.

Florence wanted to take a look at the Valletta Hospital (Sacra Infermeria) to examine her suggested structural improvements, which were finished in 1863 while the hospital continued to perform its medical functions.

Nurses and doctors were waiting for Florence when the carriage stopped at the hospital's front entrance. For them, getting to meet Florence Nightingale was a big honour. An organised greeting entailed taking a picture of all the personnel with Florence. L. Preziosi, a photographer, conducted this. She was given a tour of the hospital by the doctors and nurses, who enthusiastically described to Florence their job, the challenges they faced, the triumphs they achieved, and the miracles they were able to perform. She was overwhelmed by the tenacity of the personnel and conveyed her gratitude to them all before leaving.

As it approached Strada Reale, Dr Pisani's carriage stopped at Café del Commercio for some ices and a branded tea. The news that Florence was in Valletta spread like lightning. Although she was trying to keep a low profile, many people were observed wandering and twisting their heads from side to side to catch a glimpse of her. By this time, many people had seen her photograph in newspapers, and even hospitals displayed her photo at the front door.

With its intriguing wall scrolls, gold decorations, and fine art paintings by renowned artist Giuseppe Cali, Café del Commercio, welcomed stylish, powerful, and influential people of high standing. A table in a quiet area was set aside for Florence and Dr Pisani. The police officers had to exercise restraint to prevent the café from becoming too crowded while she was there. They were thanked by people at the other tables for all of the effort they had put into the health sector.

When the bell at St. John's Cathedral struck eleven, Dr Pisani and Florence stood up, and as she walked out of the café, gently leaning on her stick for support, people cheered, 'God save Miss Nightingale.'

Others sobbed with joy, and one woman was heard saying, 'You saved my husband.' Florence nodded, greeting the group of people who had gathered outside and were thanking her. She had become an international legend.

The carriage was waiting for them around the bend

on Strada Stretta. The horse-drawn carriage trotted through the narrow city streets and up to the bastions to shorten the distance to Floriana because they still had a long way to travel to The Forrest Hospital. The horses then accelerated to a gallop as they made their way from Floriana to Villa Spinola, also known as The Forrest Hospital, along twisting roads, arid fields, and the towns of Pieta, Msida, Ta Xbiex, and Sliema.

The Forrest Hospital was originally a residence established by the knights, but it was later converted into a forty-two bed army hospital to serve the recently opened Pembroke barracks and as a sanatorium to take in part of the overflow from Valletta General Hospital. Florence paid a brief visit since it was in her best interest to check on the hospital's efficiency and determine whether it was up to the standards set by the Royal Commission. She was pleased with the change that had been made, even though she was aware that the hospital had a sewage setback because the building's construction was never intended to be used as a hospital.

Florence needed another rest since she was feeling fatigued. She obtained a wheelchair from the hospital so she could sit down, and they continued their stroll. Together, they wandered down the Spinola promenade before Dr Pisani noticed a modest inn where they could get something to drink and take a break in the shade amid the historic buildings on the other side of the harbour. Dr Pisani opted to have a half-pint glass of beer while Florence comforted herself with a cup of tea as they both savoured the cooling breeze and the tranquilly of the sea.

The horse carriage was waiting for them to begin their journey from Spinola to Cottonera Hospital. Florence's determination was constant, and nothing was too difficult for her or Dr Pisani. He helped Florence get up from her wheelchair and into the carriage. The wheelchair was left at the inn by the coachman since it was arranged that the boy's innkeeper would deliver it back to the hospital for the cost of a penny that Florence gave him.

The carriage hurried past the villages of Sliema, Ta Xbiex, Msida, and Pieta once more via Marsa after leaving Spinola, and it then travelled a bumpy, clumsy path through the parched, golden meadows between the Marsa harbour and Cottonera bastions. The three walled cities of Cospicua, Kalkara, and Senglea—collectively known as Cottonera—are situated on the other side of the stunning harbour from Valletta, the nation's capital, and were undergoing sewer system upgrades. The population of the Cottonera region was expanding, and there were also two sizable hospitals there: the Cottonera Hospital and the Bighi Naval Hospital. The installation of new drainage systems involved disposing of sewage waste at Rinella Sea, the bastion's furthest point from the fortified city.

Reaching Cospicua, the horse-drawn carriage travelled via Kalkara alleyways that led to the harbour and up the hill to Bighi Naval Hospital. Florence paid a quick visit to this hospital because she was aware of how effectively the British Navy maintained it. She got to know the hospital's director and a few employees. The hospital had had a good reputation since 1863, when it had the opportunity to look after Queen Victoria's son, Prince Alfred, who was ill for a month with typhoid fever whilst serving as an officer in the Royal Navy. He recovered from his illness. *The Illustrated London News* of 11 April 1863 included a detailed description of how the prince was quartered and the layout of the hospital. Since then, this hospital had always been one of the outstanding hospitals in the Mediterranean.

Dr Pisani and Florence arrived at Cottonera Hospital. She received a raucous greeting. She got to know the nurses, cleaners, cooks, and doctors—the majority of them were nuns. Stepping upon the grounds of a hospital that she had established and for which she had suggested the form and planning of the units, Florence experienced satisfaction and exhilaration. The wards with large ventilation verandas, the kitchen, and stores were housed in separate blocks; the administration was in another block; separate floors were for the contagious, for the prisoners; a day convalescence room; and a ground floor for surgeries and a waiting room. She could see with her own eyes that what she had advised had materialised. It was a cutting-edge hospital that had excellent management. The patients chanted 'Long Live Miss Nightingale' as she visited them in the immaculately kept wards. She gave the workers words of encouragement and expressed her appreciation for the work they were doing.

In order to shoot a staff group picture with Florence and Dr Pisani seated on chairs in the front row, the photographer, G. Micallef of Strada Vescovo, organised the employees to assemble on the hospital's main staircase.

It was a wonderful event and undoubtedly the only chance to take a photo with Florence, who by this point was exhausted and urged Dr Pisani to get ready for their final farewell and leave. She borrowed a wheelchair to get to the horse carriage, where a doctor helped her climb on before they set out for Villa Sans Souci, where she would spend her final night before sailing back to England.

CHAPTER TWENTY-THREE

Moving On

1878, Marsascirocco

Villa Sans Souci was still dark in the early morning, but by lighting an oil lamp, Florence was able to pack her stuff and proceed downstairs to the drawing room. Except for the rooster's loud, piercing crowing sounds emanating from the farms and fields, there was still complete silence everywhere. She sat on the couch, thinking about her next moves, anticipating what the Queen might approve, and preparing the following steps for the priorities she would confront when she returned to England.

The first person to notice Florence in the drawing room was the housekeeper. Until breakfast was ready, she offered her a cup of coffee, to which Florence replied, 'Yes, please, and thank you.'

Giovanna, Dr Pisani's cousin, was in charge of securing Florence a place on a ship while she was in Malta. It was not easy to find a spot aboard a ship to leave Malta. During the hottest days of August,

Giovanna went hurrying down early mornings, afternoons, and evenings to Strada San Giovanni, with its wide, confusing stone steps and goldsmiths' shops, until the workers working the filigree became accustomed to her face and shared a smile. Then, she would make her way to *Nix Mangiare* steps, pestered by boatmen who tried to sell her a ride. Finally, reaching the admiral's office, just to be told that the steamers were full, under repair and needed to be towed, or that the next vessel was to arrive but was nowhere to be seen. After seeing that Giovanna had been coming and going for the past two days to secure a place on a vessel to Marseille for Florence, the kind-hearted admiral made a tentative reservation on the HMS *Serapis* steamer, which was scheduled to enter the harbour early in the morning and depart in the afternoon. So it happened that the HMS *Serapis* ship, carrying a consignment of army uniforms, anchored in Valletta harbour around dawn. The unloading had to be completed swiftly in order to depart that afternoon. The admiral told the captain of the HMS *Serapis* ship that Florence Nightingale would be boarding this ship this afternoon. Some adjustments were made in the underdeck to ensure she was as comfortable as possible during the voyage.

Florence entered the HMS *Serapis* at about midday and was greeted by the Scottish captain. They were merely a party of ten travellers, and the ship was loaded down with mail from Malta to Marseille. Florence was welcomed with pride by everyone on board. The ship departed Malta from Valletta harbour on one side and Ricasoli on the other. The weather in August was perfect for sailing, with gorgeous, velvety seas.

At dusk, they were on the Tyrrhenian Sea. They huddled together as travellers to offer consolation to one another and make it seem as though the time at sea would be brief. The passengers shared anecdotes; there was much literature onboard; and having access to the captain's goat on board added to the luxury of a cup of tea with fresh milk. The room on deck was occupied by Florence and a Swiss governess who was returning from a business trip in Constantinople.

'Mrs. Rose Treadway has given me a leave of absence; her children need a rest from my teaching. She will advise me by a letter if she wants me to return to Constantinople or if I wait for them to return to England to continue teaching their children.'

'Oh, Mrs. Treadway, are they going to stay in Constantinople for long? She had given me financial assistance when we were setting up the boilers at Scutari Hospital. It was so kind of her.'

'They told me that they will stay for a further three months until her husband is sent on another mission.'

'Mr. Treadway, I have met him at the general hospital as he needed treatment for his eyes.'

'Yes, I remember that incident; he had so much gunpowder in his eyes that he could hardly see.'

Then Florence said, 'I'm going on deck for some fresh air and to move around a bit.'

A flight of swallows came to rest on the rigging one evening, creating a really relaxing mood on board. For her fellow travellers, Florence signed books, documents, and letters. The captain even requested that she put her name and the date of her arrival onboard on the walls of his cabin. As they got closer to Corsica, the crewmen got weapons and Colt revolvers ready in case they ran into pirates.

When Florence arrived at the port of Marseille, the captain helped her descend the wooden gangway. Workers were busy loading and unloading ships in the busy port. She motioned for a coachman, who assisted her in climbing into the carriage and helped with her bag.

'*À Paris puis à Calais.*'

'*Oui, madame,*' the coachman replied while snatching the reins.

Florence was aware of the best places to rest, meet up with friends, and sleep. She made an effort to maintain her modesty and reserve; she detested attention, so she would be perfectly content to sip soup in an inn by herself and go unnoticed.

Florence finally arrived at Embley's Manor House. The housekeeper grabbed Florence's suitcase and walked right over to the laundry room. Florence was assisted in settling down on the couch by her sister. She was worn out. She just stood there, staring at the two halls as if it were the first time she'd seen them. Then, gently, she rose, leaning on her walking stick, and peered into the drawing room off the hallway to the right, where her father, William, was speaking with Lord Panmure.

Parthe exclaimed, 'Oh, my God, you look exhausted to death!' She took Florence's elbow to prevent her from falling, assisted her up the stairs, and led her to her room.

Parthe supported Florence in getting ready for the bathtub by helping her undress, as she was unable to do so on her own. Florence then stepped into the warm bathtub and thanked Parthe for her patience. Parthe was shocked to discover her sister in such a state—so tired and overburdened that she had grown ill, fainted and appeared lifeless.

Florence and her sister Parthe remained silent. Parthe believed that silence was the finest strategy in the face of all this exhaustion. Florence was helped out of the bathtub by both the housekeeper and Parthe, who wrapped her in a towel and assisted her in putting on her nightgown. The bed was ready for her, but as she lay down, a howl of pain erupted from the depths of her anguish, and she was left in the dark to slumber.

CHAPTER TWENTY-FOUR

The School

1878–1879, Hampshire and London

Most of the first group of nurses to enter the Crimean camp were connected to religious organisations. Although they didn't necessarily had the training, these people had prior experience helping the sick or elderly in their local communities. They came from relatively modest families, and their duties in the convents included nursing, cooking, cleaning, and laundry. However, there was a disadvantage to reporting to Florence now that she was in control. Some sisters found it challenging to follow her nursing directions rather than those from their mother's superior. The fact that the sisters or nuns were of different religious backgrounds—Catholic and Protestant—caused problems and conflicts. These disagreements and arguments even resulted in disputes over how to carry out specific tasks in front of the patient.

Florence thus listed a series of stumbling blocks

with the goal of acting on them. The action that needed to be taken was to establish a nursing education system and encourage women to become nurses, but this was a massive challenge to complete.

Women were thought to have smaller, less brilliant minds than men. The majority of women who chose to pursue education were considered to be doing so only for their own personal fulfilment or to become better wives and mothers due to the prevalent belief in 'separate roles' for the two genders. Women were never supposed to be professionals; they were only ever viewed as amateurs.

Florence accepted that women wanted to pursue a career in nursing, but she found it difficult to persuade them to do so. Their instability and unreasonableness had a long-lasting detrimental effect on Florence's viewpoint on the feminist controversy.

A movement for women's independence and higher education that began in the late 1860s was gaining strength at the time and supporting measures that would allow women to obtain advanced degrees and work in the learned professions. The issue was that Florence's temperament was now so impatient with the recommendations and guidelines of this movement, which had not even a small portion of her experience to operate as a foundation.

Florence had much higher standards. She found it difficult to comprehend why the movement insisted on using the word 'equality.' Florence never thought that being a woman made her less qualified, not because she was against women's rights in any manner. She was adamant about following in Napoleon Bonaparte's footsteps and gaining a victory over ignorance. A triumph over ignorance, which had taken control of both men's and women's minds. She was conscious that she lived in a male-dominated society where women's voices were generally considerably less heard than those of men. Despite this, she overcame it by gathering and analysing data that encouraged men to listen to her, understand her, take her advice, and be persuaded by her. Florence had the capacity to record everything, so when a man disputed her job, she could refute him with evidence and convincing arguments. Her statistics and compendium of facts might silence a minister. Her skills in giving factual information on hospital conditions, hiring, training, new hospital plans, and hospital management were in demand from leaders. For all of this, Florence wasn't looking for acclaim. She wasn't doing her job extraordinarily well; she was just doing it right.

Despite the pressing tasks and work that were piling up in London, Florence stayed inside at Embley. She did not make any public appearances, attend any events, or make any announcements. She had to focus entirely on the task at hand—establishing a nursing school.

When Florence had acquired the information, contacts, and laws required to start a school, she departed Embley. Despite her frailty, she managed to get to London with the help of individuals who assisted her on her voyage. She couldn't be stopped. The power of the Holy Spirit within her allowed her to continue the mission she had begun.

As soon as she arrived in London, she began working on the task at hand. After conferring with the supervisor of the medical training school for doctors, she proceeded with the technical aspect of the training as a curriculum for the nursing school. Probationers were required to complete a reading schedule, submit their notebooks for periodic assessment, and meet the exam requirements.

The education of nurses consisted of two phases, each of equal importance: the first required the nurse to gain knowledge, which was then evaluated by passing examinations; the second focused on the character development of the nurse, which could not be assessed by passing an exam but rather by practice on the job and in the classroom. She then appointed experienced nurses to be supervisors.

Florence stressed that nursing was both a vocation and a profession and that the student should have both the moral traits and the level of technical proficiency that are necessary for the field. The importance of commitment, composure, compassion, and maternal traits was overwhelming. Nursing, she said, 'must nurse living bodies and spirits.' It cannot be reviewed by a public examination, but it can be evaluated through continuous supervision.

In order to emphasise the idea that training nursing

schools were locations where character was to be developed, general culture was to be acquired, and a moral standard was to be learned, Florence created another milestone by referring to them as 'homes.' At the same time, the school's nurses were urged to attend church on a regular basis, read poetry, listen to music, or study an instrument. The schools' cosy atmosphere truly gave them a homely vibe.

Doctors, surgeons, and nurses were selected through interviews to serve as teachers, superintendents, and supervisors who would oversee the students' performance on the job and keep note of their accomplishments. In London's St. Thomas Hospital, the first school finally had its grand opening. Success was achieved. Florence was overwhelmed. A satisfying number of students were admitted to the school following all that administrative work. Year after year, more students joined as beginners or to finish their studies, and this number began to rise. Florence was seeing the fruits of all her efforts.

Finance was a constant difficulty. She had to turn to the Queen. The nurses had to be paid, and Queen Victoria's approval was given. Additionally, in accordance with Florence's recommendations, the Queen allocated a significant portion of the funds to the cause of having trained nurses care for the sick and the needy in their homes. This, Florence wholeheartedly accepted, would spare the hospitals time, stress, and money, and attention would be paid more to emergency casualties.

After a few years, a proposal was made with the intention of putting the trained nurse's credentials on a standard basis and granting her official recognition. When a nurse met the technical excellence in nursing criterion set by the board of members, she was allowed to have her name added to a register of nurses.

Finally, the situation in schools was taking shape. She was now more than satisfied; with the establishment of schools, standards for qualifications, and student registration, study, and qualification, nurses were now acknowledged and respected.

Florence was also in charge of hiring after a nurse graduates from nursing school; however, she had assistance from two other administrators who were constantly interviewing nurses after learning about their credentials, establishing a contract and salary, and then assigning them to the hospitals based on the need for staff in military and civilian hospitals in England or abroad in the military hospitals.

CHAPTER TWENTY-FIVE

Transforming the Dilemma

1879–1880, Marsascirocco

Dr Pisani was aware of Florence's project. They frequently wrote to each other to share thoughts, facts, and important choices. Under Miss Florence's proposals, the nursing programme in England developed gradually and successfully. Indeed, the school that was already producing qualified nurses will eventually supply nurses to Malta as a British colony.

Due to the island's financial situation, the concept of opening a nursing school in Malta was currently unfeasible. Nonetheless, as Professor of Midwifery at the University of Malta, Dr Pisani endeavoured to reorganise the School of Practical Midwifery.

Dr Pisani was scheduled to deliver the lectures at the Central Hospital, but the first challenge was the ladies who would apply for the course. Florence, who had experienced a similar situation, had warned him in advance that there wouldn't be many pupils interested in the course. In fact, Dr Pisani began giving lectures for the second time, initially to nurses and midwives who were already employed in hospitals in order to update their knowledge and abilities, but even these eventually lost interest because they were overworked at their positions due to a labour shortage and couldn't find the time to attend the lectures. The Central Hospital stopped hosting Dr Pisani's lectures.

Meanwhile, Dr Pisani at Villa Sans Souci worked tirelessly on a book about midwifery. This would be the textbook for the midwifery course and for all the mothers and grandmothers who, if they could read, assisted new mothers during childbirth in their communities as midwives without any know-how. He was primarily concerned with lowering the newborn mortality rate.

The classroom that was serving as a school was changed into a ward, leaving the school without a location because the Central Hospital was overflowing with patients. Dr Pisani persisted and made an effort to restart the midwifery school. He sent a letter to the Comptroller of Charitable Institutions asking for permission to hold a midwifery class at Villa Sans Souci, but there was difficulty because Villa Sans Souci was situated in a rural, isolated area in the south of the island.

Dr Pisani persevered and even offered his horse-drawn carriage to transport the pupils, but this would all depend on the number of students since the carriage could only fit four or five. In partnership with the Comptroller of Charitable Institutions, Dr Pisani declared that a midwifery course would begin in October. He picked up the applications at the Strada Merkanti Post Office and brought them to Villa Sans Souci for review. Four of the six interested students were foreigners working as nurses for the British Army or British Navy, while the other two were Maltese. The Maltese applicants were sadly rejected by Dr Pisani since their résumés demonstrated a lack of literacy. So, the horse carriage would transport four international students who were already qualified nurses from Valletta to Villa Sans Souci in Marsascirocco twice a week. The class would be held in the drawing room. If the weather permitted, they were to spend their break time outside in the garden or on a walk in the countryside. Dr Pisani, the new students, and the Comptroller of Charitable Institutions had everything planned out and agreed upon. The theory classes would be held at Villa Sans Souci, while the practical technicalities would be held at the Central Hospital on an anatomical model, which practice had produced prejudices and scruples, and had disappointed Dr Pisani since he could not do proper practical teaching.

The housekeeper put together a trolley that day with tea, coffee, and toast with jam. Dr Pisani transformed the living room into a tiny classroom by adding a blackboard to one wall and a table with his books and demonstration items for midwives. The four experienced adult learners would bring their experiences to class, and Dr Pisani's goal was to teach them in a way that would allow them to instantly apply what they were learning to their everyday activities in order to further their careers.

The horse carriage's wheels rumbled forward to the mansion's entrance. The four students were Eliza, Beatrice, Margaret, and Anna. Dr Pisani greeted them warmly.

Their shared experience as nurses quickly sparked candid conversations about medical issues. They all related their experiences in Malta and England. Beatrice was not only inspired to become a midwife but also to earn a doctorate degree. She had previously worked in Germany at the same Kaiserswerth Krankenhaus as Dr Pisani and Florence Nightingale. All of them received encouragement from Dr Pisani, who was also willing to support them in achieving their professional goals.

The entire course would take two years to complete. Dr Pisani's interaction with the students had grown familiar. Eliza and Margaret were employed by the Birgu Naval Hospital. They were both vivacious and daring women with a solid background in the medical field. Settling on this island, with their families while enrolled in the midwifery course, they used to bring their young children into the care of Cettina, the housekeeper, who was maternal and devoted by nature. They used to spend the majority of their playtime in the Marsascirocco countryside or in Villa San Souci's garden if it was not predicted to rain.

Beatrice and Anna were single. They were still in

their late teens and preferred to divide their time between work and recreation for the time being. Since they were already under a lot of stress from their nursing duties due to the war, it was crucial to find time to unwind after a long day.

Dr Pisani also has his own methods of unwinding. He was too preoccupied with his job to consider romance or marriage. He spent his free time working in prominent positions in the medical field. Though he admitted to having some fun while studying in England and Germany and that he once fell in love with a German student in the same classroom, his discipline of concentrating on the studies and experiments remained the most important way he spent his time.

Dr Pisani, now in his early fifties, had developed a sense of tranquilly that he pursued after a day of pressure at the Central Hospital, thanks to the gorgeous landscapes and peaceful surroundings at Villa Sans Souci and the spacious residence. Having these students at his property was also an opportunity for him to relax after working in busy hospitals. He enjoyed imparting his expertise to the students because he understood that they were the nation's future and that it was essential to cram as much knowledge as possible into their heads in order to maximise both their individual accomplishments and the gains the country would make in the field of health.

The smartest student in the group was Beatrice. Dr Pisani was very happy with her desire to train as a midwife and eventually register in a doctoral programme. She was the one who talked to the Professor the most. She stayed at Villa Sans Souci for longer hours, learning everything Dr Pisani could impart. The housekeeper occasionally made her dinner. She was fashionable all around, intelligent, elegant, and well-groomed. Dr Pisani could recollect her mentioning the name Mary Clarke once during their talk as she related her past and her family tree, which had its origins in England before moving to France.

'Oh, absolutely!' She finally confirmed, 'Mary Clarke, also known as Clarkey, is my aunt.'

Dr Pisani's friendship with Beatrice grew stronger after he told her that he knew Mary Clarke well through Florence Nightingale in Paris and that he even stayed overnight as a guest at her residence.

Yet one morning, when she arrived for the lesson, she appeared confused, and Dr Pisani sensed that something wasn't right. Her cognitive thinking was foggy, making it difficult for her to focus. After the class, she was leaving with the others with the justification that she wasn't feeling well. Dr Pisani begged her to stay and inquired as to how he might assist. Beatrice sobbed when she sat down and told him she was pregnant while fighting back tears. Beatrice had dated a Navy man whom she had met in a Valletta pub. She had also taken care of him after he had been injured during a fight among drunken friends. She had been sharing a room with him that the navy had provided for them, but now that she was expecting a child and he had left for an extended mission as a navy officer, Beatrice felt entirely alone.

Dr Pisani's altruism offered Beatrice the opportunity to transfer her belongings to Villa Sans Souci. Here, she would not feel lonely. Cettina would attend to everything she required.

She stayed in the same room Florence Nightingale occupied during her stay. Beatrice offered to have her pregnancy stages included in the practical course as a gesture of her thanks, allowing all the students to gain real-life experience and knowledge. She even offered to give birth in front of her classmates.

As the course continued, Beatrice's pregnancy also made progress. She served as the model. She was the subject of the course's practical part. She would wear a silk gown when she entered the drawing room. The door and windows would be closed, and Beatrice would remove her gown, followed by a detailed description of her body's growth by the students and Dr Pisani. In order for the students to feel Beatrice's movements and hear the sounds of the foetus, they were allowed to touch her. In this training, genuine involvement was essential; yet, at the Central Hospital, such interaction was not only not permitted but also censored. Even a portion of the theory side was concealed, and Dr Pisani's books' illustrations were blue-penciled. How could one learn effectively if crucial information was withheld? This 'taboo' was ignorance, to put it simply.

Dr Pisani kept up the professional manner in which he delivered the lectures. The practical portion of the course, in which Beatrice was the main character, served its objective. They only attended practical sessions on the anatomical dummy twice at the Central Hospital, which they felt was a complete waste of time. However, as Dr Pisani explained to them, the Comptroller of Charitable Institutions had to record their attendance for the purposes of the final qualifications.

Months had passed, and Beatrice was about to give birth. She was put in one of the bedrooms, where Dr Pisani and the other three students helped her through the pain of giving birth. It was an unforgettable experience for everyone. A healthy boy was delivered, and Beatrice had already decided on the name George for him. George looked perfect, even though he was still covered with amniotic fluid, and the happiness and fulfilment of Dr Pisani, Beatrice, and all those present could be seen in the glint in their eyes.

The midwifery final examinations were to be held at the Central Hospital's administration. Dr Pisani was confident that this group would pass with flying colours, stating,

'Finally, I've made it; this group had the courage to train as midwives, and with some qualities, I risked my reputation for the practical portion of the course offered by Beatrice, who served as a role model for the entire class to overcome the lack of practical training considered to be scruples.'

His publications on midwifery were in print and would be used for the upcoming courses that would be given at the University of Malta, as agreed upon by the Dean, the Chancellor of the University, and the Comptroller of Charitable Institutions.

A short distance from Villa Sans Souci, at the Chapel of St. Peter of Verona, the baby, named George, was baptised in front of Beatrice and Dr Pisani's housekeeper without disclosing the identity of the father.

CHAPTER TWENTY-SIX

Beatrice

1881–1882, Marsascirocco and Valletta

Beatrice was always clear to Dr Pisani that she did not want to continue living in 'hiding' and would rather return to Paris with her child, George.

George's father seems to have disappeared overnight. The letter she sent to his parents in England was marked 'return to sender, wrong address,' and she never received a response from him.

She was still youthful and vivacious. She didn't mind travelling because she knew where she had to go. The university would be nearby if they moved in with her aunt, Mary Clarke, who would undoubtedly welcome them with open arms. Dr Pisani's heart suffered at this decision because he was now beginning to feel like a father to Beatrice. However, he knew where Beatrice would be and would continue to help her with her studies. He could pay a visit to Clarkey's house in Paris to see both her and her child, and he would also be there to attend the German Medical Society's congress in Paris, so they would still be in touch, even though he would miss them both growing up. Undoubtedly, the housekeeper would yearn for George as well. She had been his babysitter since his birth.

The day arrived when Beatrice, a midwife employed at the Central Hospital, resigned in order to leave the island after spending over three years there. All of her and George's things were carefully packed by the housekeeper. There was undoubtedly a melancholy atmosphere inside the mansion. Pisani had a busy surgical schedule, yet he made the decision to delegate control to other surgeons on that particular day. He would miss Beatrice and her son. They gave Villa Sans Souci a family-like atmosphere that Dr Pisani yearned for, but as was already mentioned earlier, his professional obligations never gave him the opportunity to form relationships or a family. He had now played the part of this father for almost three years, caring for and shielding Beatrice, instructing and learning alongside her, and then George, who was promptly cradled in the arms of all. They would leave a void in the hearts of everyone in the mansion.

The thoughts persisted in the back of his mind as he accompanied Beatrice and her son to the harbour. The vessel was already loaded. One of the most beautiful ships of the period was the French steamer *Sinai,* and she occasionally sailed into the ports of Malta. While the captain was inspecting the deck, Dr Pisani came over and gave him some cash. He wanted the captain to make sure Beatrice and George were well taken care of and secure. The captain would assign someone to escort them to Paris as soon as they reached Marseille. Three goats were brought on board to provide milk for the crew and the twenty passengers.

A large crowd had gathered at the waterfront, and because he was a well-known physician and professor, he tried to keep his emotions in check. With the assistance of an Indian crew member who carried their bags down the hallway, he witnessed Beatrice and her son board the ship as he cast his final glance at them. Dr Pisani and Beatrice exchanged a quiet *au revoir* as Beatrice turned to face him.

A sense of emptiness filled Dr Pisani's heart as he climbed into his carriage and gave his coachman the order to gallop away from the crowds of people by heading to 'Ta Liesse,' where he found a quiet spot and stood in the carriage watching the *Sinai* divide the blue waters and leave the harbour.

It was late evening when Dr Pisani returned to Villa Sans Souci. He was drunk. His coachman took care, holding him by his arm and yelling at the mansion's entrance for Cettina, the housekeeper, to assist him. Cettina dashed outside and helped the coachman carry Dr Pisani into the drawing room. She had never seen the Professor in that state. The coachman calmed her down; he understood that the Professor had endured too much heartache and that the drinking had resulted from the Professor's inability to control his suppressed emotions.

Dr Pisani awoke the following morning bewildered

and perplexed, reflecting on Beatrice and George's journey. He was distressed by the mansion's abandoned state of bareness. Still wearing his long white nightshirt, he left his room. As he descended the stairs, Cettina jumped in shock, spilling the milk she had just gotten from the

goats in the stables and raced to the kitchen to fetch a cloth to clean the floor. She had never witnessed him in such a ghostly state.

Dr Pisani instructed the housekeeper to inform the coachman that he would not be going to work and that he needed to speak to them as he entered the kitchen to prepare breakfast. There had to be a decision, so Dr Pisani announced it while everyone was seated at the breakfast table.

'I'm going to Paris,' he declared. 'Beatrice and her son will require help. Her aunt, Mary Clarke, is too busy running her salon to care for George. Since I am familiar with Mary Clarke's character and the child is unfamiliar with the citizens of Paris, I am certain of what I am saying. In the meantime, I'll wait for the German Medical Society conference's scheduled dates in Paris. I'll return to Malta and then to Paris as often as necessary until Beatrice graduates. She assured me that she would return to Malta as soon as she graduated because she adores the island.'

The *Ottawa*, a four-masted iron screw steamer, entered the Maltese harbours. It came with a cargo of cattle and uniforms. It took a day and a half to unload, and Dr Pisani and the other twenty-four passengers had to wait another day for it to be cleaned and ventilated before boarding. The odours left by the animals were unpleasant.

The *Ottawa* set sail for Liverpool via Marseille, where Dr Pisani would debark. He knew the voyage by now. Dr Pisani stayed in the company of the other passengers. Even more, he offered them a medical checkup and gave them treatment and wellness advice. Even the crew and captain, who also need a comprehensive examination of their health, highly appreciated his contribution.

The voyage on the *Ottawa* was a tranquil one in the summer weather. The pirates in the Corsican region were the only source of commotion in the Mediterranean. When the ship approached the dangerous radius, revolvers and rifles were ready and set aside to be distributed to the crew and some of the passengers.

At this hour of darkness, the sea was calm and completely silent. A boat with a small, faint light coming from it was seen approaching, but it had passengers on board who were all gathered on the deck, and crew members could be heard issuing commands to maintain discipline. In addition to the vocal commands, the whispering of whips could be heard as it drew nearer. It was a slave ship bound for Algiers, full of terrified passengers who were wailing in terror as well as little children.

Dr Pisani continued to focus on the boat. He had a lot of thoughts and shivered with anxiety, but the captain called to offer him some tea, and his worries were quickly dispelled by the captain's maniacal laughter in response to one of the passengers' jokes.

The final few knots appeared to be too long for Dr Pisani. He remained on the deck, worn out and depleted by his thoughts. He saw that the Marseille harbour lights at night were getting bigger every day, indicating that they were getting closer to the land.

CHAPTER TWENTY-SEVEN

At Marseille

1882–1883, Marseille Harbour and Paris

The *Ottawa* entered the harbour of Marseille. A sense of anxiety filled the heart of Dr Pisani. There was a lot of movement on the harbour coast and Dr Pisani noticed a vessel being towed and manoeuvred towards the docking yard. He glanced at the captain of the Ottawa and asked him whether he recognized the vessel.

'It's the *Sinai*,' he prompted while trying to manoeuver the *Ottawa* into its berthing place.

Dr Pisani's heart sank. Something happened to the vessel *Sinai*, but what? He dashed downstairs for his belongings and jumped onto the quay, almost falling into the sea. He ran hastily towards the admiral's office at Marseille to question him about the *Sinai*. A small crowd chanting, *'Les pirates l'ont encore fait, ils ont pris nos bien-aimés,'* had already gathered in the area. Confounded, Dr Pisani entered the gathering and moved people out of his way as he climbed to the entrance of the admiral's office. Because he could comprehend

French, he could understand the cries of the audience. Angry and frustrated, he banged on the closed door, accompanied by some from the crowd, who immediately followed what he was doing. They demanded an answer as to what happened to the passengers on board the *Sinai*.

A port official from the office emerged through the window. Overlooking the crowd, he declared that the corsairs had raided the ship *Sinai* and taken not only the cargo but also the crew and passengers to Algiers under the protection of the French Army. They would work for the French Army instead of being sold as slaves.

Dr Pisani was enraged by the news; he wanted Beatrice and George to return to Villa Sans Souci, where they would be completely protected. He hurried up to a horse-drawn carriage that was standing outside the admiral's office and gave the driver the command to drive him to Paris.

The distance seemed to take forever. The only certain source of assistance for him as he raced against time was Ms. Mary Clarke. She must have political connections that might help her get her niece Beatrice and her son George back.

The barouche went faster than ever before, galloping to its utmost at the opportunity of good terrain, as the coachman was aware of the emergency. Dr Pisani had recounted all that had happened and showed him a picture of Beatrice and her son, George, taken at G. Micallef at Strada Vescovo, a month before their departure.

On the fifth night of continuous travel, the carriage arrived at the Avenue des Champs-Élysées and proceeded towards Mary Clarke's mansion. The coachman waited to see if Dr Pisani's desperate knockings with the gleaming brass were answered, before assisting him with his belongings. A faint glow could be seen approaching from behind the stained-glass panels of the entrance. The door opened on the brass chain first, revealing a pair of startled eyes before the person quickly unlocked the door completely. Dr Pisani never expected to see Florence Nightingale there at that hour, and neither did she. Florence recognised his troubled and frightened state; they sobbed together before Florence led the way inside to the drawing room and shut the door behind them.

After a busy night in her salon, Ms. Clarke was dozing off in her bedroom. Dr Pisani revealed immediately to Florence the account of Beatrice, Clarkey's niece, and how she had a boy named George, their journey, and their tragedy. He was sobbing like a child, sitting on the first canapé he fell into, his head slumped down, almost touching his knees. He knew Mary Clarke would think he had shown a lack of responsibility by allowing Beatrice to embark on this journey, and he was feeling too awful about it. Now he intended to do everything in his power to secure the return of Beatrice and her son. He would seek Mary Clarke's assistance in the hopes that she could speak with some lawmakers, who may send a representative to look for them.

Florence Nightingale happened to have travelled to Mary Clarke as she was meeting the Sanitary Commissioner to the Government of India in Paris, as health affairs in India could hardly have been more discouraging, and she was bitterly disappointed. She still had a lot on her mind, and work never ceased, on the contrary, it accumulated, especially in countries such as India. The difficulties were enormous, owing to the extremely poor level of the Indian Medical Service.

This story, though, was suddenly the focus of her attention. She admitted that she and Mary Clarke were already aware of Beatrice's relationship with the navy man and the fact that she was the mother of a son. Beatrice had revealed everything to her aunt, and Florence knew about this. They were looking forward to meeting Beatrice and George, but a tragedy had occurred, and Mary Clarke needed to know all that had happened.

Dr Pisani could not lift himself out of the canapé; tiredness took over, and his eyes closed. Florence stood by his side, then brought him a wet cloth to wipe his forehead and face, swiped his lips with her finger with water, and dragged a dining chair over to sit by his side. She was accustomed to having restless nights, and this one was no different.

At the break of dawn, carriages were heard rumbling down the Boulevard Montmartre, and market sellers howled with what they had for sale. Sounds of strong metal bars hitting, clunking, and hammering were heard in the far distance. The Eiffel Tower was at an advanced stage of construction. Paris was remarkably busy at the time, with the construction of the Opera House, the Métro, and the Basilica, so lots of people were settling in Paris because of its progressive projects, optimism, and elegance.

Mary Clarke, who was still in bed, was informed of the news by Florence. Confounded by the information, Miss Clarke rang the bell to summon the butler as she hurriedly wrote a note to Albert Grevy, a temporary Governor General of Algiers who was well-known to her. The butler quickly left with the note in hand.

In the meantime, Mary Clarke and Florence went down to the drawing room, only to learn that Dr Pisani had rushed away with her butler to deliver that note.

At noon, Mary Clarke was on the brink of taking the carriage to go by herself to search for Albert, when the butler and Dr Pisani dashed through the open door with a note confirming that Albert Grevy would be sending Prince Napoleon, together with two other officials, to Algiers. They would go straight to the French Army camp, where they were supposed to find both Beatrice and George.

'I'm going with them,' said Dr Pisani.

'Take care, and we will wait for any news from you,' uttered Florence.

At port Le Havre, Dr Pisani, Prince Napoleon, and two other officials boarded the *Weser*, a paddle gunboat that happened to be required for service in Algiers by the French Army. The *Weser* parted the seas with its bow for sixteen days, which were accompanied by wind, rain, and shine. They had all sorts of weather, as it was that time of the year when the instability of meteorological conditions was experienced on the open seas.

The Algerian coast was completely in the hands of the French government. The *Weser* entered Port D 'Algiers with the Senior Port Admiral and other French officials waiting for them to dock. The Algerian mooring men were prepared to tie the mooring ropes to the old, disused cannons, whose barrel ends were buried inside holes dug in the ground and whose posteriors protruded out of the ground to provide a sturdy mooring station. Mooring ropes were thrown onto the quay by the crew from the bow and stern. Dr Pisani set foot on the African continent for the first time in his life.

CHAPTER TWENTY-EIGHT

The Rummage

1883, Algiers

By the time Dr Pisani arrived in Algiers, the population of the French was just over two hundred and ten thousand, and that of other foreigners, such as Spanish and Italians who immigrated to Algiers, was nearly the same figure. This, besides the Muslim indigènes who were practically over eight hundred thousand. The French seemed to have done their best to try to bring order to the way the country operated, but it was not enough, and the Muslims had their own ways of managing their traditions in everything they did.

As soon as Prince Napoleon entered the camps, he was promptly met with respect by the French soldiers. There, in Algiers, discipline predominated more than anywhere else on the globe because the French were well disciplined and had outstanding soldiers. The only way to begin the search was to visit these military bases among the soldiers and ask around for Beatrice and George, showing them the picture in the hopes that they were still there and hadn't been taken by the Muslims. Prince Napoleon realised that this would take a long time, so he appointed soldiers to help and sent them into each camp, calling out the names of Beatrice and George. Days went by, and those names remained unanswered. Dr Pisani was exhibiting the picture to everyone he saw, but all he received in response was a head shake from left to right or individuals turning their faces and leaving. Dr Pisani was reassured by Prince Napoleon that they would be located, but it would take more time because the French population in Algiers had grown exponentially.

After finishing the search in the northeast of Algiers, they moved towards the west, where a younger generation of soldiers was occupying the military camps and where Alsatian-Lorraine refugees, counting around five thousand, settled on the ground of Algiers after their land was taken by Germany.

The search for Beatrice and George proceeded among all those people. Dr Pisani was adamant that he would cuddle them both once more; in fact, he felt stronger and more determined than ever. The majority of the lengthy travels were made on foot or with the aid of a horse, donkey, or cart. It was impossible to walk because of the tremendous humidity, heat, and stinging sand that poked one's face and body like small needles when the wind decided to switch from a zephyr to a stronger force.

They made the decision to pitch a tent in the

Muslim area one night. They had to take a rest and resume at dawn. The next military camp was not far distant, according to Prince Napoleon. While making a fire on the sand to scare away critters and cook something to eat, Prince Napoleon noticed a lonely horse approaching them. It had a saddle on its back, so Prince Napoleon quickened up his steps until he could grab the saddle and clamber aboard. Without the reins, it was challenging to control and steer, but Prince Napoleon was an expert rider and was able to accomplish it.

After giving the horse some water to drink, Prince Napoleon let down the straps that were constricting its abdomen and swung the saddle onto the sand. Something fell from beneath the saddle, catching Dr Pisani's attention. He hurried over to grab a lace handkerchief embroidered with the initial B.

'Beatrice, we're near,' he said as his eyes grew brighter and he lifted the handkerchief towards Prince Napoleon's face. Prince Napoleon examined the beautiful lace of the handkerchief in his hands.

'We should wait till daylight because we all need a rest, but it's Maltese lace, and she should be at the next camp we visit.'

Dr Pisani nodded in agreement with Prince Napoleon's remarks and then laid down on the sand beneath the tent, waiting for the sun's first rays while holding Beatrice's lace handkerchief close to his face, imagining the scent of Beatrice. A tear streamed down his cheek, and he felt bad for leaving her to her own devices, but a stronger sensation quickly took over within, a feeling of determination, a feeling of conquering the circumstance. The Arabic tongue rang out throughout the tents at first light. Prince Napoleon calmly picked up the weapon and exited the tent. As he looked around, he noticed a group of men encircling their small tent, all of them were wearing the traditional Arab garb of overlapping cloths covering their bodies and faces. As a display of goodwill, Prince Napoleon commanded his military authorities to give the men some water. They only spoke in their native tongue, but Prince Napoleon had a representative who could translate what they were saying.

'Tell them that we're here on a mission to find missing people, maybe they can help.'

They appeared to be interested in helping them, so Dr Pisani showed them the picture of Beatrice and George. The sight of people's pictures on a card astounded them. They chuckled at the image before turning to face Dr Pisani and requesting that he accompany them. In response, Prince Napoleon raised his weapon and fired a shot into the air while aiming at the red sky, which was still changing into its morning hues. They hastily backed away from him as they frantically tore the photo to pieces and yelled obscenities in their native tongue. As they moved on to the next tent, Prince Napoleon urged everyone in the company to keep going. Every stride seemed heavy and strained as sand filled their shoes, leaving a deep cavity in the sand. The burning rays revealed the tired and exhausted looks on everyone who was there.

By noon, voices in the distance could be heard on the breeze, indicating their approach to a camp. Dr Pisani watched his shoes getting coated in sand, dusted, and then covered in sand again as he walked with his gaze fixed on the ground to keep the sun out of his eyes. Then, as he turned to face the horizon, he noticed a row of tents and some people heading out in the distance. Dr Pisani's tired feet were spurred to accelerate his pace by a sense of comfort that Beatrice and George might be nearby.

The names of Beatrice and George could already be heard being yelled out by the soldiers who arrived first. The camp had become chaotic. They were informed that the Muslims had just frightened and horrified several of the camp's female residents, some of whom had been removed. Dr Pisani's heart plummeted as he heard the words, but then he heard heavy breathing. 'I'm here,' Beatrice shouted, using her last gasp and trying to catch her breath again.

She came running from the desert towards the camp. Dr Pisani begged Beatrice for George as his eyes began to well up with tears. 'They took them from here; while I was performing my midwifery duties, I left him with a woman. When the Muslims arrived, they violently pulled some of us away, including the woman holding George in her arms.'

Dr Pisani and Beatrice sobbed uncontrollably. For George, the situation was hopeless. Prince Napoleon made an attempt to console them, but Dr Pisani snapped. He ran into the desert while holding Prince Napoleon's weapon, shouting and firing erratically at the Muslims' direction of travel. He broke out in tears and knelt on the hot sand.

The suffering was intense. The search had partially failed, and Prince Napoleon had to inform General Governor Albert Grevy of everything before they could board the next ship to France. Dr Pisani and Beatrice were disoriented and anxious as they boarded the ship to escape the awful country of Algiers, where they had been separated from George.

CHAPTER TWENTY-NINE

Back in Paris

1883–1884, Marsascirocco and Paris

It had been a month since their return to Paris. Giovanna, his cousin, received a letter from Dr Pisani informing her that he would soon be in Malta. Beatrice made the decision to stay put with her aunt rather than go on a trip. When she felt more whole but not entirely whole—wholeness would never be possible after losing a son—she would resume her life and finish her doctoral studies at the University of Paris.

Dr Pisani would spend time in Malta and travel to Paris to help Beatrice with her life and education. He wouldn't desert her; rather, they agreed that she would maintain a steady pace in her studies so that, when she was done, she could go back to Villa Sans Souci and work as a doctor in Malta.

At Villa Sans Souci, time seemed to have stopped. Everything was left the same as Dr Pisani had left it when he departed. Giovanna, his cousin, got to know the whole story from Salvatore Luigi himself on his arrival.

'Letting them embark on that journey is shameful and disgraceful. Allowing a young woman and her son to leave alone. In the eyes of the French authorities, you're reckless,' Giovanna said emotionally.

'Stupid ideology!' Dr Pisani exclaimed, 'get out of my house.'

Giovanna tossed the kitchen towel onto the bench, scooped up her bag, and dashed away with the coachman.

Dr Pisani desired to remain on his own; he desired to regain his energies and resume where he left off in his career and writings. He was sorry for how he had treated Giovanna; her remarks had scratched an unhealed wound. After all the upheaval, he wanted to attempt to find some peace with himself, get plenty of rest to replenish his body, and find some balance in his life once more.

Dr Pisani never ceased writing to Beatrice, even if it took her longer to respond because she was still recovering. He even addressed some of his letters to Mary Clarke, asking her to take care of Beatrice.

A year later, Pisani was appointed to the new position of Chief Government Medical Officer, the highest-ranking medical practitioner on the island. He continued to write about diseases and outbreaks as well, and he created a thorough report on the cholera pandemic that year that included a synopsis of earlier epidemics in Malta and Gozo. He suggested that the government raise local public health standards, including providing clean water, sanitising working-class housing, and expanding the sewage system to rural areas.

Dr Pisani had achieved great success in his medical profession. The elite respected him. Villa Sans Souci was once again entertaining lords, ladies, nobility, professors, and generals. Champagne and scotch were once again served in the drawing room, and in the garden, laughter aired the rooms and garden gazebo, eradicating the monotonous ambience that whispered in the home, but not in the deep scars behind Dr Pisani's heart.

After three years, Dr Pisani made the decision to schedule a second visit to Mary Clarke in order to spend more time assisting Beatrice as she completed the final of her coursework and would shortly receive her PhD. Through letters, analytical reports, and detailed medical papers that he had written for his own research, he had consistently helped her with her studies. Beatrice would finish her studies and return to Villa Sans Souci with Dr Pisani to be employed as a medical officer at the Military Hospital at Zabbar Gate.

Dr Pisani was now on his way to Marseille to reach Paris. Even on the ship, there was always a need for his services. One of the passengers was carrying a child at an advanced stage of pregnancy, and he assisted her in every way he could with the restrictions he had on board by checking her out, giving her advice, and helping her in any way he could.

After reaching Marseille and starting the horse-drawn carriage ride to Paris, he stopped by some of his friends along the route, always sharing his experiences, his research, and his studies while attempting to pick up more medical information from other doctors.

When Dr Pisani arrived at Ms. Clarke's house, it was midnight on the seventh day of the horse-drawn carriage journey. Unexpectedly, he discovered the door open, and a priest seated on the couch, leaning over the Bible that was resting on his knees. He was approached by a butler, who recognised him and motioned for him to join him upstairs.

Beatrice was found lying in one of the bedrooms, her eyes empty and her skin ghostly white. Dr Pisani gazed at Ms. Clarke in stunned silence. Dr Pisani wanted to provide his doctor's assistance, but Mary Clarke requested that he refrain. Beatrice had been sick for two days, and it had all started with a bite of an Ornithonyssus bacoti (or tropical rat mite) when she trod on a mouse while walking to university one early morning at the crack of dawn.

Beatrice's bedside was attended by Mademoiselle Schultze, the top medical doctor from the Paris faculty. Holding Beatrice's frozen hand, Dr Pisani knelt down near the bed. The room was dark and silent until Beatrice let out one final gasp before her head dropped from the pillows. Mademoiselle Schultze kissed her on the forehead and gently closed Beatrice's eyes.

Dr Pisani's heart ached so much that it was unbearable. He was in a lot of pain, and the entire room could hear his cries of sadness and anguish. Mlle Schultze embraced Dr Pisani and held him close to her as he rose up, and together they exited the room and proceeded downstairs to make place for the priest to do the ritual anointing. Mary Clarke remained in the room, contemplating writing to Beatrice's mother to inform her of her daughter's death.

There were no words spoken because even one word would have been inappropriate in a situation like this. In that difficult, painful moment, the sobs, the inhalations, and the tears meant everything. The world seemed to be closing in on Dr Pisani after losing not just George but now also Beatrice.

Dr Pisani felt Miss Florence's hand caress his shoulder, and as he gazed up at her, he sobbed bitterly.

There was considerable activity in the house at morning. All the funeral preparations were being handled by undertakers, who also picked up the body, prepared the coffin, prepared the horse-drawn hearse, prepared the church, and finally prepared the 'picnic wagonettes' for the cemetery park wake.

It was normal practice for people, particularly Parisians, to go outside of the city for the day to visit a sizable park-like cemetery in the countryside. Funerals were frequently all-day events in Paris, so mourners prepared a picnic meal. They put miniature lemon cakes and exquisite gammon sandwiches in a basket to be consumed on lawn blankets. They had plenty of time to think back on their loved ones who had passed away and their ancestors who were interred there. Dr Pisani found it unusual, yet he was obligated to observe these traditions.

The jangling and clanging could still be heard in the distance. The Eiffel Tower was almost finished. The city's commercial district was bustling. In the heart of Paris, Florence was holding talks with Lord Salisbury, W.H. Smith, the Secretary of State for War, and representatives from India. Her thoughts were on India. There, the Sanitary Board was finally established in each province. Finally, Florence's plan was operating, if not completely, then at least somewhat. Many things still needed to be done, and given her advanced age, every delegate was anticipating her ideas. The funeral for Beatrice necessitated rescheduling their meeting in Paris. The unshakable support and inspiration Florence provided for Dr Pisani were more constant and robust than ever. She was aware that he felt motherly comfort in her, and a genuine love grew.

CHAPTER THIRTY

The Last Quests

1883–1884, Paris and London

Following Beatrice's funeral, Florence went ahead and met with the Indian representatives as planned. In addition, she and Dr Pisani were talking about the plans, projects, and schemes that would be implemented in India. Florence wanted Dr Pisani to be involved as well, so she was able to extricate him from the depressing situation life had thrown him into and persuade him to start studying and analysing work tasks that would aid his mental wellness while he was in Paris.

On the third day of the meeting, Dr Pisani formally acknowledged his attendance. They were a wonderful value when working together because their lifelong efforts and accumulated knowledge were now providing great benefits for nations like India. India was developing its infrastructure, creating sanitary educational initiatives for the traditional population, and constructing hospitals. Even though she and Dr Pisani still had a lot of work to do in India, it would all be consulting work because of their status, knowledge, and wealth of experience.

'I ought to promote more reforms in India,' insisted Florence. 'Even though the conditions for British troops in India have improved, I still need to exert pressure on the government to advocate for preventive hygiene in the Indian army and at home.'

The head of the Indian delegation said, 'The Indian administration viewed you as an intrusive person who was demanding such reforms.'

'I would continue to advocate for a complete overhaul of India's hospital administration system. I would keep pushing for improvements in hygiene.'

At the conclusion of these meetings, Florence and Dr Pisani wrote a memorandum outlining the various programmes in India, placing a high priority on sanitation, and stating that a portion of the taxes paid should be used to address problems where a village lacked proper drainage systems, a clean water supply, or a way to properly dispose of its waste; if there were diseases like cholera and others, all of these issues should be of urgency.

While all of this was going on in India, innovative measures were taken in England to develop the district nursing system. This initiative immensely assisted the community and lessened the burden on hospitals. It was developed on the notion that women should have access to education so they can become qualified to impart basic domestic health principles to village mothers. Florence, who was adamant that this was the quickest way to develop hygienic education in every nation, said that the village was to be treated as a unit and that the ladies were to work with the mothers of the villages rather than lecture them.

Additionally, schools were established at a number of hospitals in England and other nations. Being formally registered and placed on the registry of nurses after successfully finishing their studies will protect the public from receiving any services from nurses who might be dishonest or incompetent.

The Victorian Era Exhibition's organisers contacted Dr Pisani and Florence a month after their arrival in England. In honour of the illustrious Florence Nightingale, this exhibit featured a segment that highlighted the development of professional nursing. The event was remarkable since it coincided with Queen Victoria's Diamond Jubilee. However, Florence refused to give them a portrait of herself or specific Crimean War mementos. Dr Pisani persuaded her to hand them the Steell bust and a few other objects. The organisers were appreciative of the gifts, and Dr Pisani gave them the necessary information so they could be displayed next to the objects.

The evening of the exhibition turned out to be a magnificent one. The bust and relics of Florence Nightingale were treasured as holy items by the masses. Flowers had been arranged in front of her bust. She had successfully completed a lifelong ambition.

After a few days had passed, Dr Pisani left Florence a message on the coffee table in the Embley drawing room. It served as a farewell as well as a summary of his admiration and gratitude for her. Dr Pisani believed it would be better to tell her in writing rather than in person because he wasn't sure he'd have all the words.

He crossed over to Calais and made his way to Paris. He made a brief visit to the main post office to drop off a note for Prince Napoleon, telling him to get in touch with him at the Malta address if he heard anything about George.

All day, George was on his mind. Although his life had been destroyed, he never lost hope or faith.

On his arrival in Malta, mayhem ruled inside the hospitals. Malta had become overcrowded with the military, navy, and common people. The hospitals for the proletariat were insufficient. His reports of constructing a new hospital remained just plans, and nobody took any action as there were insufficient financial resources.

Despite the challenging hospital environment, Dr Pisani's fortitude remained unwavering. He was able to perform surgeries despite the considerably worse conditions he was in.

The nursing school facility, or at least some rooms to serve as such, was still missing from the island, and the majority of the nurses were nuns who had completed their education at Rome's Santo Spirito Hospital in order to meet Florence's standards. Their work was crucial, especially when you consider the poor conditions of the public hospitals.

Dr Pisani would walk to Valletta after a long day of work. The statue honouring Queen Victoria's Golden Jubilee had just been moved from the harbour to Republic Square gradually on large carts drawn by six horses, where it stayed unveiled until the celebration day. More than ever, people of many ethnicities were occupying the streets of Valletta, whether they were there for business, pleasure, or any other reason.

Dr Pisani always took the same route through the city. He took coffee at the Cafeteria del Commercio before going to see his cousin Giovanna, with whom he had restored his acquaintance after Beatrice passed away. She resumed assisting him with his routine housework.

At the time, Villa Sans Souci was being redecorated with new drapes, carpets, and additional furniture for Dr Pisani's collection room and study. Giovanna was taking care of all the interior details and overseeing the gardener and housekeeping to ensure that Villa Sans Souci was always welcoming to visitors and would never dull again.

Dr Pisani commissioned Edward Caruana Dingli to create a painting of Beatrice and George based on the sole photograph that photographer G. Micallef had reproduced—a copy of the one that had been destroyed by Muslims in Algiers. Dr Pisani sought to avoid any questions by keeping the portrait hidden and out of sight of any visitors. The ideal spot was on the wall of his bedroom.

Despite Villa Sans Souci being in stunning condition and occasionally welcoming guests, Dr Pisani's heart was still in dire need of healing.

Letters from Florence, Ms. Clarke, his contacts in other countries, and his friends in Malta arrived at the post office, but Dr Pisani was constantly hoping to hear from Prince Napoleon with the joyful news of Beatrice's son. On Beatrice's deathbed, he promised her to find George no matter what.

CHAPTER THIRTY-ONE

Who Was It?

1891, Malta

Dr Pisani went downstairs the morning after his house was broken into and found the police officer half asleep. He begged him to go home to rest, and in the meantime, he would send his coachman to handle the windowpane repair.

The policeman agreed and said they had no idea who had done such a thing, but he instructed Dr Pisani to go to the Casal Zejtun Police Station to inquire about the situation.

After eating breakfast and easing his throat with freshly ground, fragrant African coffee that tasted of roasted coffee beans, he read some of the letters he had collected from the Strada Merkanti post office the day before. Then he informed the housekeeper that because he was off duty today, he would be going to Casal Zejtun police station and returning.

The sergeant welcomed Dr Pisani to his office and briefed him on the case. The individual who destroyed the lower window panel and escaped could not be located after extensive searching. The sergeant apologised for his lack of information and promised to watch the villa in case the thief tried to enter again.

Dr Pisani put on the hat, thanked the police officers, and went away. As he returned to Villa Sans Souci, he pondered if the burglar had just intended to smash the window and flee because he had damaged the lower window panel, preventing him from reaching the lock. He accelerated his steps as he became curious about the circumstances.

When he got to Villa Sans Souci, he discovered the coachman taking measurements for the window panel's replacement. Dr Pisani entered the drawing room right away; he could still hear some glass fragments crunching beneath the soles of his shoes. The housekeeper was about to start cleaning the area with a broom when Dr Pisani noticed a folded piece of paper behind a side table, next to the damaged panel. He pulled the side table away from the wall so that he could lean against it and pick up the folded paper. He unfurled it and saw the torn-up picture of Beatrice and George, which shattered his heart. The letter read, '*Je suis arrivé, je suis à Alexandra Hotel Strada Marina, Sliema.*'

Dr Pisani implored the coachman to drive him to Sliema, completely forgetting about the windowpane. After a few early morning neighs and the tumble of hooves preparing for the voyage, the horses' leashes were jerked to give them direction, and off they ran, rolling over grass and urban dirt cobblestone pathways, the carriage rattling and squeaking.

The horses kicked up a cloud of dust as they passed through Casal Zejtun, Paola, Marsa, and turned towards Pieta. They also passed through Msida, where they had to slow down because the construction of the new church for St. Joseph, which was by this point nearing completion, had caused congestion in the small alleyways. Then they galloped through Ta Xbiex and as they approached the Alexandra Hotel, the reins were set loose to slow the speed since these routes were busier. Dr Pisani lost patience and jumped onto the sidewalk when he noticed the carriage was wedged between two other carriages and a street vendor's donkey was angry and neighing violently in the middle of the passage. '*Ha nimxija*, I'm going on foot,' Dr Pisani exclaimed at his coachman.

Rushing his steps and running simultaneously, he arrived at the Alexandra Hotel. He felt confused because he had no idea who to approach or what to say to the receptionist, but once inside, he had a good look around. He spotted a Muslim woman sitting by herself at a corner table with a delicate, fair child next to her, while a few other people were drinking coffee in the lobby area, which is located across from the entrance hallway.

If she was waiting for him, Dr Pisani indicated it by extending his neck. She stood up, nodded her head in agreement, and Dr Pisani walked over to her table. '*Bonjour*,' she said.

Dr Pisani gazed into the boy's eyes, which were bright and filled with tears ready to fall down his cheeks. The boy innocently broke the numbness that had settled between them by saying, '*Je suis George*,' he said with a cheerful smile that lit up his entire face and showed how happy he was. Dr Pisani was overcome with emotion and could not hold back his sobs. He hugged George while wiping away his tears and feeling his heartbeat. He had a tonne of questions for him, but now was not the time or place for them. He was ecstatic, and so he gestured to them to follow him as he left the hotel and headed towards his horse-drawn carriage. George and the Muslim woman could only communicate in French. '*Aller à la Villa Sans Souci?*' George asked him. '*Oui,*' prompted Dr Pisani.

When they got to the villa, the housekeeper was busy polishing the brass lion heads on the doorknobs and the brass hinges. She halted her duties and turned to see who was getting out of the carriage. She saw Dr Pisani leaping out and turning to help a boy. Dr Pisani turned to face Cettina with a broad smile and said, 'George.'

Cettina threw down her cleaning rags and dashed over to George to hug him. She moistened George's shoulder as she sobbed excitedly, showering him with all the affection she had been holding back for him since their last encounter.

'Oh, my God, you managed to find him,' she said to Dr Pisani.

Dr Pisani then extended his arm to assist the Muslim woman in exiting the carriage and said, 'Thanks to her, but we still must hear all the story. They speak only French, so I will translate for you what happened.'

Cettina eagerly entered the kitchen to make some snacks and drinks as everyone sat in the living room conversing in French, a language she knew little about other than a few basic expressions from her time spent weaving at a French family's home.

The woman from the Muslim community, Asmaa, began telling Dr Pisani what she knew about George. She was one of Saddam's wives, the leader of the Muslim organisation where George ended up after being snatched from his mother. They initially believed that the woman holding George in her arms when they were evacuated from the camp was his biological mother, but she refused to care for the child any longer after making it plain that it was not hers. Saddam told Asmaa to take care of his upbringing, as he looked like a healthy boy and could become a good man.

Upon entering the tent, Saddam flung some documents and maps out of his hands. After Asmaa made Saddam's ceremonial tea, bullets were heard far out in the desert, prompting Saddam to irately leave the tent and flee with a few of his cronies across the sand carpet.

Asmaa gave the infant some milk while he was in his cradle, and once she was able to put him to sleep, she began to pick up the teacups and examine the trash. She picked up the papers her husband had thrown away and discovered the ripped picture. She assembled the image and flipped it to look at the reverse, which bore the stamp of G. Micallef Photographer, the shop's address, the names Beatrice and George, and the year the photograph was taken.

Asmaa began covertly arranging to return George to his family. She had to wait until the child had grown up, so she kept the photo tucked away under her blankets. Asmaa simply carried out Saddam's instructions to take care of the child because he was no longer interested in her and had other women to amuse himself with.

When Asmaa decided it was time to take George out of Algiers, she requested assistance at a French camp, telling the story to one of the Generals who had been told by Prince Napoleon about the missing George. He was eager to assist Asmaa, so she was informed of the day and time a vessel would leave Algiers, and she made sure she and George were on board.

When she arrived in Malta, she found Maltese locals willing to assist her when she showed them the photo with the photographer's address on the back. It was Sunday, and the shop was closed, so she and George went for a walk around Valletta and then stayed at the Alexandra Hotel till the next morning. Asmaa found living in Valletta to be amusing as she observed all the merchants' selling rolls of curtains made of silk, linen, and brilliant Mediterranean colours, as well as delicately woven lace.

However, George was the priority because he was the reason she was there. On Monday morning, they went to G. Micallef first. Asmaa and George entered the shop and placed the ripped picture face down on the counter.

She pointed at the name written on the back of the photo and said, '*Je veux l'adresse de cette personne,*'

The proprietor of the shop responded, 'I don't know; I am not understanding.'

A customer who was considering purchasing a magnifying glass said, 'I am understanding. I speak French; she asked you for that person's address.'

The photographer was initially hesitant to give her the details, but when he heard her say, '*Le garçon est perdu*, the boy is lost,' he handed her a paper with the address written on it. Asmaa took the paper and hired a horse carriage that carried her to Villa Sans Souci, but she was terrified when she saw the massive villa in front of her. She was at a loss for what to do, and so they went back to the Alexandra Hotel. Then, in the wee hours of the morning, she informed the hotel front desk that she had to leave immediately because a ship was coming in with a member of her family on board. She requested a horse-drawn carriage to pick her up, but she instructed the driver to take her to Marsascirocco instead because the ship would be entering the harbour from the south.

When the coachman arrived at Marsascirocco, it was completely dark, and he felt strange leaving a woman there. However, he saw a dim light on the horizon and thought it might be the vessel the woman was waiting for—perhaps a fisherman. He thanked her for the money she gave him, which was more than the cost of the trip, and galloped off.

Asmaa ventured out into the night on her own and made her way up the hill to the villa. As she got there, she could hear the horses in the stables neighing and braying, obviously alert to her presence. Asmaa cracked the window-glass with a stone she had picked up from the path outside and hurled the folded message and photo towards the furniture in an effort to get it to its purpose as quickly as possible. She knew that the message would surely get across this way. She hurriedly walked towards some woods to remain hidden and kept walking in the stillness and darkness until she heard the horses' galloping hooves, at which point she entered a field and hid beneath a carob tree. To make it difficult for anyone stealing a peek from any window of the house to see her, she kept on walking under the trees at the side of the path. She persisted in walking towards Paola until she saw a bread baker who was travelling to Marsa while hauling wood in his cart and offered her a lift. It took her until first light to return to the Alexandra Hotel, where she discovered George waking up.

While Asmaa continued to tell Dr Pisani the entire tale, George asked Cettina to show him around the house.

He chose an apple from the kitchen, bit into it with

gusto, and then ran outside to see the garden. He ran towards the limestone gazebo and climbed up on its wooden benches, stamping his feet to maintain balance. In a flash, he was running along the path between the trees. When he returned inside, he headed upstairs, and Cettina followed him, her legs more supple than ever and yelling, 'Be careful, be careful, don't run in the stairways.' He was unable to understand Cettina's words. When George stopped to look at some of the furnishings, paintings, or photographs that he found most appealing, Cettina would descend and gaze him in the eyes, mumbling in her limited and weak French, '*Une chose merveilleuse,*' while she panted. As George ran faster, reaching the upstairs corridors, he peered inside each room as if looking for something or someone. Cettina followed him, adjusting the beds that George climbed on, and closing the rooms after he left. George then peered into Dr Pisani's bedroom. He saw the painting there, fixed his gaze on it, and then sprinted down the stairwells while yelling, 'Dr Pisani, Dr Pisani,' with Cettina trailing behind and yelling, '*Lente, lente.*'

George, panting and thrilled, came to a halt at the door of the drawing room, where Asmaa and Dr Pisani were still present. His gaze caught Asmaa's and then Dr Pisani's, and he asked in a squeaky innocent child's voice, '*Où est ma mère?*'

GLOSSARY

Maltese words

Aljotta – this is a Maltese traditional soup made of onions and fresh fish.

Barrakka – Barrakka are gardens along the bastions of the city that originally were built by the Italian knights in 1661.

Bigilla – broad bean and garlic dip.

Gallarija - a distinctive component of Maltese vernacular architecture, the *Gallarija* (plural: *gallariji*), is an elaborate closed wooden balcony.

Galletti – the Maltese word for water crackers.

Ħa nimxija – I'm going on foot.

Ħierġa – she's going out/on her way out.

Indjani, Indjani, intlejna – Indians, Indians overcrowded us.

Karozzin - the *karozzin*, a historic form of transportation in Malta, consists of a carriage drawn by a horse or horses. It used to be well-liked for everyday use. Now one finds it only for tourist tours around the capital city Valletta and the old city of Mdina.

Luzzus – a traditional fishing boat of the Maltese islands.

Minestra – a traditional vegetable soup.

Rubble walls – in Maltese *'Ħitan tas-Sejjieħ'*, are a prominent and essential element of the Maltese rural environment. The history, wisdom, and expertise of our ancestors' agrarian communities are reflected in these classic agricultural structures.

Remise building – the traditional cart or horse carriage room, like today's use of a garage.

French words

Aller à la Villa Sans Souci? - going to Villa Sans Souci?

À Paris puis à Calais -to Paris then to Calais

au revoir – goodbye

Bonsoir – Good Evening

Bonjour – Good Morning

Je lève mon verre à la liberté – I raise my glass to freedom.

Je suis arrivé, je suis à Alexandra Hotel Strada Marina, Sliema - I have arrived, I am at Alexandra Hotel Strada Marina, Sliema.

Je suis George - my name is George.

Je veux l'adresse de cette personne – I want the address of this person.

Le garçon est perdu – the boy is lost.

Lente, lente – slowly, slowly

Les pirates l'ont encore fait, ils ont pris nos bien-aimés- the pirates did it again, they took our loved ones

Où est ma mère?- where is my mother?

Oui – yes

Oui, madame – yes, ma'am

salle-à-manger – dining room

Sans Souci – carefree/without worries

Une chose merveilleuse – a wonderful thing

Italian words

Nix Mangiare – deriving from the Italian words '*niente da mangiare*' meaning nothing to eat. Maltese beggars used to stay in these stairs begging passers-by that they are hungry.

Tartana della Neve - the tartana is a sailing vessel equipped with a single line mast with a lateen sail sometimes flanked by a jib. Della Neve means of the snow. This kind of boat used to carry snow from Mount Etna to Malta.

REFERENCES

Alldridge, Lizzie, Florence Nightingale, Frances Ridley Havergal, Catherine Marsh, Mrs Ranyard ("L.N.R.") (London; Paris; New York: Cassell & Company Limited, 1890)

Andrews, Mary Raymond Shipman, A Lost Commander: Florence Nightingale (Garden City, New York: Doubleday, Doran and Company, 1929)

Cassar, Paul, Medical History of Malta (London; Wellcome Historical Medical Library, 1964)

Cook, Edward Tyas, The Life of Florence Nightingale, (London: MacMillan & Co. 1913)

Edge, Fredrick Milnes, A Woman's Example and a Nation's Work; a tribute to Florence Nightingale, (London: William Ridgway, 169, Piccadilly, 1864)

Galea Francesco, The First Photographer in Malta, (Times of Malta article)

Gordon, Richard, The private life of Florence Nightingale, (London: Heinemann 1978)

Great Britain, War Office, Copy of all official reports of the hospitals at Scutari, Kululee, Abydos, and Smyrna, since February last (London: HMSO 1855)

Great Britain, War Office, Scutari, &c., hospitals: return

to an address of the Honourable The House of Commons, dated 14 May 1855; — for, "Copy of all official reports of the hospitals at Scutari" (London: 1855)

Kinglake, Alexander William, The Invasion of the Crimea, (Edinburgh: Blackwood 1899)

Lord Houghton, The Life and Letters of John Keats, (Edward Moxon amp Co., Dover Street 1867)

Nash, Rosalinda, A Short Life of Florence Nightingale, abridged from The Life, by Sir Edward Cook (New York: The Macmillan Company, 1925)

Nightingale, Florence, Notes on Hospitals (London: Longman 1863)

Nightingale, Florence, Army Sanitary Administration and Its Reform under the late Lord Herbert, (McCorquodale & Co. London, 1862)

Nightingale, Florence, Florence Nightingale to Her Nurses, (MacMillan and Co. Ltd, 1914)

Nightingale, Florence,The institution of Kaiserswerth on the Rhine, for the practical training of deaconesses, under the direction of the Rev. Pastor Fliedner, embracing the support and care of a hospital, infant and industrial schools, and a female penitentiary (London : printed by the inmates of the London Ragged Colonial Training School, 1851

Nightingale, Florence, Letter of Advice to Bellevue, (1911)

Nightingale, Florence, Life or Death in India, (Spottiswoode & Co, London 1874)

Nightingale, Florence, Notes on Nursing, What it is and What it is Not, (D. Appleton and Co. New York, 1860)

Nightingale, Florence, Notes on Nursing for the Labouring Classes, (London, Harrison 1861)

Nightingale, Florence, Observations on the evidence contained in The Stational Reports submitted to her by the Royal Commission on the Sanitary State of the Army in India, (Edward Stanford, London 1863)

Nightingale, Florence, Rural Hygiene, Health Teachings in Towns and Villages, (Spottiswoode London, 1894)

Nightingale, Florence, To the Probationer Nurses of the Nightingale Fund School at St Thomas' Hospital, (London, 1886)

Nightingale, Florence, Sanitary statistics of native colonial schools and hospitals, (London, 1863)

Nolan, Jeannette Covert, Florence Nightingale, (New York: The Junior Literary Guild and J. Messner, inc. 1946)

Pope-Hennessy, James, Monckton Milnes, The Years of Promise 1809-1851, (London Constable, 1949)

Report to the Right Hon. Lord Panmure, G. C. B., &c., Minister at War, of the proceedings of the Sanitary Commission dispatched to the Seat of War in the East, 1855–56 [electronic resource] by Great Britain. Sanitary Commission Dispatched to the Army in the East (1855–1856), (London : printed by Harrison [for] H.M.S.O. 1857)

Report to the Right Hon. Lord Panmure, G.C.B., &c 1855- 56 printed by Harrison & Sons 1857

Scutari, &c., hospitals : return to an address of the Honourable The House of Commons, dated 14 May

1855;- for, "Copy of all official reports of the hospitals at Scutari, Kululee, Abydos, and Smyrna, since February last."

Simpson, M.C.M (Mary Charlotte Mair), Letters and Recollections of Julius and Mary Mohl (London : K. Paul, Trench & Co, 1887)

Strachey, Lytton, Florence Nightingale (London: Chattu and Windus, 1938)

Tooley, Sarah A. Southall, The Life of Florence Nightingale (London: New York: Cassell and Company Ltd, 1916)

Unknown (by A Lady), Kaiserswerth deaconesses, including a history of the institution by Kaiserswerth Deaconesses (London: Joseph Masters, 1857)

Viscount, Esher, The Letters of Queen Victoria (London: John Murray, 1908)

Woodham Smith, Cecil, Florence Nightingale (New York: McGraw-Hill Book Company, 1951)